MORNING, NOON
AND NIGHT

MORNING, NOON AND NIGHT

EROTICA FOR COUPLES

EDITED BY
ALISON TYLER

Published in the United States by Cleis Press, Inc., 2246 Sixth Street, Berkeley, California 94710.

Printed in the United States.
Cover design: Scott Idleman/Blink
Cover photograph: Digital Vision; B2M Productions; Vincent Besnault/Getty Images
Text design: Frank Wiedemann

First Edition.
10 9 8 7 6 5 4 3 2 1

Trade paper ISBN: 978-1-57344-821-5
E-book ISBN: 978-1-57344-835-2

For SAM.

Contents

INTRODUCTION: SEX AROUND THE CLOCK

You've heard the concept of christening a brand-new house? Making sure you've fucked in every possible corner—in the shower, on top of the washing machine, in the cedar closet, outside against the woodshed. (Oh, God, that woodshed.) Well, my man and I took this concept a step further. We wanted to fuck around the clock—christening every hour of the day in a brand-new way. And do you know what we learned? There is something sublime about sex at sunrise, something otherworldly about a two a.m. bang on the beach. And when you figure out how to slip away for a noontime quickie, you will discover that lunch will never be the same again.

The authors in *Morning, Noon and Night* rose to my challenge of making sex around the clock a unique endeavor. From noon to midnight and back again—any way you tick the minutes—the stories chronicle a twenty-four-hour schedule of sultry, slippery sex. This collection contains tales of shift changes and office briefings, of missed appointments and erotically enhanced commutes.

We begin with a "Four a.m. Wake-Up Call" by Jax Baynard, because I am often up at four. In fact, it's four a.m. right now. Somewhere. No, wait, it's "Five p.m. Somewhere," which is the name of Kristina Lloyd's exquisite snowed-in story about a couple who run out of gin but manage to make the first non-alcoholic martini of all time. (At least, in any erotic story I've ever read.) I'm proving my point here, which is that you can dive into this day-in-the-life (or day-in-the-*lives*) schedule at any hour and come away with a hot little sojourn into serious, silky sex.

Whether you're flipping the pages or running the ball of your fingertips over your screen—whether you're in Central, Mountain, or Daylight Savings Time—get ready to fuck your way around the clock.

Morning, noon *and* night.

XXX,
Alison Tyler

P.S. And since there aren't enough hours in the day for fucking—there's actually a twenty-fifth story in the book. Thanks to Aisling Weaver for her frisky flasher.

24/7

Aisling Weaver

*F*ifteen years later and they still ignite each other. It happens
in the morning. She looks over her shoulder and he has to
bend her over the kitchen counter. Later in the living room.
He snaps the newspaper just so, and before he can find the
funnies they're scattered on the floor and his pants are around
his ankles.

Any time of day or night. Their love fuels their lust. Tonight
it's the storm. To the soundtrack of thunder he spreads her. She
strokes his stubbly jaw, wraps her legs around his waist and he
strokes his cock into her.

FOUR A.M. WAKE-UP CALL

Jax Baynard

I rolled over and looked at the clock: four a.m. My husband was asleep next to me. Despite having a husband, I hadn't gotten any lately. He was stressed about work. On him it didn't show, but I lived with him and he'd been under so much pressure he was going a little out of his mind. So I could hardly add to it by being demanding. And yet. I was starved for cock. There was no delicate way to put it. I was married to the best one I'd ever come across. I thought about it all the time, dreamed of it, yearned for it and fantasized about it, but I wasn't getting it. I was having orgasms, of course, about three a day, but it was getting to the point where it seemed like work more than fun. Still, if I didn't have them, I went a little bit out of my mind. I had hit that age where, unexpectedly, I suddenly had something in common with every teenage boy on the planet: I wanted sex, and I wanted it more or less all the time.

I lay quietly and listened to the even rasp of his breathing. I thought about waking him up and begging for it, but no matter how creative I was I knew he wouldn't appreciate the suggestion. His alarm was set for five a.m. His flight to Tallahassee was at eight and his presentation at three.

My pussy was not at the top of his priority list.

Deciding to make myself useful, I slipped out of bed and padded barefoot down the stairs. I flipped on the lights in the kitchen. Airline food, never good at its best, had only gotten worse—unless it was nonexistent altogether, in which case the preoccupied business travelers could just go hungry. I fished some nori out of the cabinet, found some day-old rice in the fridge, added sugar and vinegar to it and chopped up some vegetables. The carrots were definitely phallic and the cucumber almost didn't make it into his lunch at all. Only eight years of fairly domestic bliss kept it in his lunch and out of my cunt. I sliced the sushi rolls into even pieces, put them into a container, added an apple and a PowerBar, shoved the lot into a brown paper bag and put it by the front door where he couldn't miss it (I hoped) on his way out.

Then, not wanting to go back to bed, I wandered into the library. I sat in the leather armchair and splayed my legs. I let my hand drift through the already wet, dark curls. I wasn't up to much effort, but I knew if I just lay back and thought of his cock and the things he used to do to me with it, and let my fingers travel back and forth over my clit, it wouldn't feel like so much of an effort in a few minutes.

He cleared his throat. "Hey," he said. In the dim light of morning, I could just make him out standing naked in the doorway.

"Hey back," I said, dropping my hand, embarrassed for no reason I could think of.

"Oh, don't stop," he said. "I got up early to give you a going-away present."

A quivering sensation began in my stomach and spread downward. "I thought people got coming-home presents," I said, fighting to keep my voice even.

He smiled, moving toward me, his cock fiercely erect, upright against his belly. "If things go well, you can have one of those as well." He knelt between my legs, placing his palms on my inner thighs as if to hold me in place, which was funny. A whole lot more than wild horses couldn't have moved me from the spot.

"Missed you," he said, tonguing me, starting just above my asshole and licking all the way up to my clit. "Sorry," he said. "My fault."

It felt so good just to have him touching me, much less running his tongue all over the most sensitive spots on my body. I was squirming, greedy, wanting everything in the first instant. I was babbling, sex words, love words, pleas. He made a firm point with his tongue and stabbed it into me. I jerked and twisted in his grasp. "I need your cock," I said.

"Really?" he inquired politely, but he was sweating, a fine sheen across his chest. "I thought I might do this for a while. Remember the first time I did this to you? You liked it a lot then..."

"I want your cock," I said. *"Please give me your cock."*

"Oh, well," he said, all teasing, false modesty, "If you put it that way." With a quick, hard jerk he pulled me off the chair and into his arms, my thighs over his, my back braced against his arms. The sweet, aggressive slide of his flesh into mine made a keening sound start in my throat. I tightened my arms around his neck, sucking on him, his neck, his jaw, wanting it to feel as good to him as it did to me. He thrust into me, controlling it, refusing to move faster. And then he stopped, hard and throbbing inside me. I wailed in protest, but if he wasn't helping, it wasn't that easy to get purchase. I tried to knock him over so

I would be on top, but he withstood me easily. "Hold still," he said in my ear, low-voiced. "I want to suck on your nipples."

He proceeded to, until I was a mindless bundle of nerves, grinding my hips down on him, trying desperately to rub my clit into his pubic hair so I could come. He held me off just enough so I couldn't. "Easy, baby," he said, but he was panting. "Let's make it last awhile."

"Fuck you," I said. "Plane to catch, remember?"

"Oh, that," he said, as if he hadn't a care in the world, after six long weeks, except having his thick, hot cock inside me for as long as possible. "Forget the shower." He licked sweat from my collarbones. "I'll go like this and the other husbands will be jealous. I'll have the smell of your pussy all over me and it will drive them crazy." His hands tightened on my hips and he resumed thrusting, faster now, less in control.

I was done with words, beyond them. They were gone, like someone I used to know. There was just this, the powerful surging of his body into mine, over and over and over again. I raked my nails down his back, something for him to think about on the plane. In answer, he dumped me on the floor, pulling out and shoving back in, lost himself, as if his body had finally remembered that sex was the best stress reliever on earth. Waves roll across the ocean for a long while before they crest and crash onto a long shore. I came, but for the first time in my life I barely noticed: it wasn't the point. I had what I wanted: his cock inside me, his climax breaking him apart so he lay shuddering against me in the aftermath. He forced himself up, though, arms trembling. "I have to shower. Do you want to be back in bed?"

"Liar," I said. "In a minute."

He'd heard that before. He got me into his arms and, staggering slightly like a drunk, carried me up the stairs and put me back to bed. "Have a good trip," I said, reaching up to kiss him, my hand on the back of his neck the last thing to leave his body as he turned away. I felt sleepy, sated with happiness, made of nothing but air and light.

FIVE A.M. WALK OF SHAME

Dante Davidson

When Gennifer walked down the street toward Max, he couldn't help but notice that she was wearing the exact same outfit she'd had on the night before. Generally speaking, he was not the type of guy to pay such specific attention to what a woman was wearing, but this was a noticeable creation. Through the plate-glass windows of the café, he spied her dark wine-colored satin corset fastened over a white peasant blouse and a short, flirty black-and-red velvet skirt. Her black fishnets were noticeably ripped and her boots had high, spiky heels. This was not your average coffee bar attire, nor was it your average five a.m. attire.

Not unless you were doing the Walk of Shame.

He started to laugh under his breath as she entered the shop. Gennifer didn't even look his way. With her head held high, she strode behind the counter—heels click-clacking on the tiled floor—and tied one of the little black-and-white aprons around her slender waist. Five a.m. is early to most people, but to a coffee shop crew, Gennifer was actually a half hour late. Max had covered for her, starting the various jobs that she did by his side on a daily basis.

Without a word, she began the normal prep routine, turning on machines, checking supplies. He noted when she bent down to look in one of the low mini refrigerators that her skirt was torn in the back. Three sterling safety pins held the fabric together, gleaming under the lights.

He blinked, knowing exactly what it would take to rip the fabric like that. He could imagine tearing the skirt, shredding the back along the seam. He could almost hear the sound of the fabric giving way, a small shriek of submission from both the skirt and the girl wearing the skirt.

His cock twitched.

Gennifer turned around suddenly, catching him staring, obviously lost in his filthy thoughts. Her ivy-green eyes narrowed, and he felt himself blush. Without a word, she stood and moved past him, and when she did, she made sure her hip brushed his growing erection. Holy fuck. He had to suck in his breath to avoid moaning.

"Some night, huh?" Max managed to choke out as she moved past.

"Straight out of an X-rated movie," she said, flicking on the various devices that would soon fill the shop with the aroma of rich, dark coffee.

He looked at her face. She still had remnants of the previous night's makeup. Her eyes were lined with kohl, her lids smudged with a plum-colored shadow rich with glittery pigment. Her lips were stained dark berry red. When she bent forward over the cash register, he saw a spot where she'd been kissed hard enough to leave a bruise deep in her cleavage. That sent him once more into fantasyland, spiraling into visions of climbing on top of her, tearing her shirt open, biting and kissing her small, ripe breasts.

His cock was a throbbing, demanding being at this point. The shop wasn't even open for business and he couldn't wait to get off—in two ways. Gennifer moved by him once more, and this time she actually let her fingertips graze the outline of his hard-on through his jeans, but she did so in a casual, almost accidental manner. He could almost hear her taunting voice in his head.

This time, Max did groan and press back against the counter. He couldn't help himself.

"You getting an eyeful?" she asked, and her voice was so raw with sexual need that Max considered fucking her right there, against the coffee canisters. "You want to see everything?" She started unlacing the corset top, but Max had the wherewithal to stop her, grabbing her wrist and pulling her to the unisex bathroom. He flipped on the fluorescent light and turned the lock.

There were a lot of things he wanted to say to her, but he couldn't call her a cocktease, because Gennifer was already hitching her skirt to her waist and bending over the porcelain sink. Max sighed when he saw she didn't have any panties on. He had the presence of mind to think that she'd actually gone knickerless with her skirt torn like that—and wondered if anyone else had spied her pink. He slid one hand between her legs and found that she was dripping wet. Was she *already* wet from their encounter or *still* wet from the night before? He didn't care. He tore open the front of his jeans and thrust his cock against her naked skin, not in her, not yet, just on her. So he could feel her heat.

Gennifer had the corset off and was working on the blouse.

"I can't believe you actually went through with it," Max said as he finally slid his cock inside her.

"A dare is a dare." She smiled mischievously at him in the bathroom mirror.

He remembered the previous night as if in Polaroid images, still frames frozen in time. Over tequila shots, he and Gennifer had discussed the customers they served on a daily basis—the ones who came to get their regular dull coffee to go with their regular dull lives, and the ones who seemed like they might have a little kink in them. *The walk of shamers*, Gennifer called them. Those were the patrons she liked best, enjoying spinning stories about what their night-befores might have been like.

"That Flo," Gennifer said, "she always looks as if her man has been keeping her up all night long." Flo was a hall of famer walk of shamer. Sometimes Max had a difficult time meeting her eyes when he served her, she was so obviously recently fucked.

He and Gennifer talked their way through the various customers. The couple was mildly tipsy, drinking on the floor in her living room, teasing each other in a light manner until he said, "You're one to talk, you know. You get fucked six ways to Sunday each night. You simply polish up nice and pretty in the a.m."

"I don't always have to," she'd taunted. "I can be as sloppy as your favorite walk of shamer." This was a girl named Megan who came in several times a week looking obviously mussed. Gennifer said that Megan would be lost if she didn't have at least one visible hickey.

"Oh, really? What would it take?"

"What do you have to give?"

She'd actually gotten up and nudged him with her bare foot, playing rougher until he'd stood up with her.

"No," she'd told him. "Wait here."

She'd sprinted down the hallway, and he'd heard her rumbling around in her bedroom. He'd drained the last of his glass of tequila, imagining what she might be doing out of sight from him. When she'd returned, she was dressed in a whole new outfit, having discarded her standard T-shirt and cut-offs in favor of what he could only describe as Mardi Gras on acid—a red-and-black slutty creation that made his cock immediately hard.

Something about the clothes had changed her attitude as well. Gennifer had play-punched his shoulder, then gone on her tiptoes to ruffle his shaggy blond hair.

"What do you want?" he'd asked, gripping her wrists to stop her.

"I don't want just a 'slept in' look," she'd told him. "As if I missed the alarm clock and had to rush. Anyone can have bedhead. I want to look like I've been really fucked. Good and proper."

"Don't I do that every night?"

He knew he did. She'd never complained before. He'd taken her in the shower, on the sofa, outside on the balcony. He'd spread her pale pussy lips and eaten her out for hours, had sixty-nined with her until she'd creamed against his lips in the sweetest way. But he'd never played the way she pushed him next.

"I want you to fuck me so people will know," she'd said, pulling away from him and running to her bedroom. *So people will know.* How was he supposed to do that? The question in his head, he'd chased her, sprinting down the hall, reaching for her at the doorway, his hands on her skirt. She'd pulled, and he'd torn the fabric, not fully, not demolishing the short skirt. But torn. The sound of the fabric rending had startled him, and he'd stopped still, his heart racing.

"Max," she'd said. "Don't worry so much." And she'd put his hand back on the skirt and shown him what she wanted. "Tear it."

He'd carried her to the bed, tossed her on the mattress and

gripped the skirt in both hands. The tiny tear had given way to the gaping rip that she'd done her best to pin together this morning. Safety pins couldn't hide what he'd done. What she'd wanted him to do.

The thoughts of the previous evening made him harder than ever. He parted her legs and slid his cock in her hole. She lowered her chin and closed her eyes. He watched her expression change in the mirror.

Everything had happened in a rush. But that didn't mean he couldn't recall his hands working over her fishnets, creating those gaping, naughty holes. He'd demolished her shirt, pulling buttons off the bottom in his haste to remove the blouse, had nipped and bitten at her skin hard enough to leave the bruises she wore proudly today. They'd done it like beasts, hungry and loud, in a way they'd never fucked before. When he'd come on her ass, even his semen had felt hotter than usual.

And then, surprising him, she'd pushed him out of her bedroom, out of her apartment. "I'll see you in the morning," she'd told him, kissing his lips, lips that felt battered. "Get some sleep."

Some was the operative word. He hadn't gotten home until after two. Getting to work on time had taken Herculean strength.

And that had led them to this point, with him fucking her against the sink in the bathroom of the café where they both worked. He'd never seen a sexier walk of shamer, and he told her so.

"I can't take all the credit," she whispered as he nailed her. "You did the work on the skirt." He thought of how he'd torn it off her the night before. He'd never thought she'd have worn the thing again, especially to work.

She pulled off him, surprising him, and went on her knees

on the bathroom floor. He sucked in his breath as she sucked in his cock, licking the head and then working her mouth up and down the length. She was drinking her own juices off his rod, and he was in a state of bliss watching her. What had gotten into his girlfriend? He couldn't imagine—but he relished every second.

"Remember how you shredded my hose?" she taunted, taking a breath. He did. He'd used his fingers to tear gaping holes in the stockings, considering the fishnets dead on arrival. She'd infused them with life for at least one more day. Still, he was shocked that she'd taken the dare to this level.

She stood and then pushed herself up on the edge of the sink. "Finish them off, baby. Tear them to shreds."

He ripped the stockings just like she'd asked, and then he plunged into her again. She wrapped her thighs tight around his waist, and he knew he would come like that, with their bodies sealed so tightly together. He watched in the mirror as he hoisted her in his arms, palming her naked asscheeks as he bounced her.

"Next time, I want you to tie me down with my stockings," she said, and he knew her words were going to make him come. "You'll rip every bit of my clothes off me, and you'll use the shreds to tie me in place."

"Yes," he said, his voice reduced to a harsh whisper. "Yes, yes, whatever you want."

He came hard inside her and he felt her body responding, his orgasm tripping her own climax. He could hear the noises of the machines in the café, and he knew he had to go back to work, that customers would be coming before too long. "Are you really going to wear that all day?" he asked, watching as she did her best to resurrect her attire. Without the corset, she looked more refined. If she didn't turn around, the customers wouldn't know the skirt was so worked over. "I never would have thought you'd go through with this."

"You ought to know me better than that, Max," she said.

He tilted her chin upward and kissed her lips. "I do now," he told her with a smile.

"You *think* you do," she countered. "But you have no idea what I'm going to dare *you* to do tomorrow."

SIX A.M.
COFFEE

Heidi Champa

Looks like you had a rough night, Elisha." Aaron handed me a cup of coffee as soon as I walked in the door.

I groaned, the most I could manage at six in the morning, my throat filled with sweet, creamy coffee.

"The bachelorette party got a bit out of hand. You can't say no to the bride. You know that. And when there are two of them, well, let's just say there was a lot of peer pressure involved. They are like bridezilla squared. Besides, once we got in the limo, there was no stopping them."

"So, what did you guys do? Was it a dancing and getting drunk on Cristal kind of night, one club after another?"

I didn't respond, so he kept going. He was laughing before he even started his next sentence, clearly amused with himself.

"No, wait, don't tell me, you went to a strip club. That would explain the glitter on you and the reason you smell like that raspberry lotion you claim to hate so much."

He laughed harder, but it died in his throat when he saw the look on my face. I gave him a sheepish grin, as I had no idea what else to say.

"Oh my god. You did. You did go to a strip club, didn't you, Elisha?"

"All right, yes. We went to a strip club. Ranna and Jasmine wanted to go. What was I supposed to do?"

I expected him to say something negative, to tell me how stupid places like strip clubs were. Although I knew he'd been to a number of them in his time. I'd offered to go with him plenty of times before, but he'd always reserved those clubs for guys' night. Jasmine had made it clear that all of us were going to the club before I could even protest their plans. But, if I was being honest, I didn't want to say no. I was curious to see what all the fuss was about. And turned on by the thought of it all.

Aaron sat back and sipped his coffee, his blue eyes softening around the edges.

"So. You. At a strip club."

I sighed, leaning my chin in my hand. I was in no mood for one of his little diatribes on the best of days. I certainly wasn't ready for one at six in the morning and after the night I'd had.

"Aaron, I'm tired. Just say what you want to say and get it over with. Judge me, I don't care."

He set his coffee cup down and tapped his fingers on the table. I closed my eyes, waiting for his response. He cleared his throat, and the first words out of his mouth were barely a whisper.

"Did you get a lap dance?"

I opened my eyes and looked at him, expectation all over his face.

"What?"

"You heard me, Elisha. Did you?"

"Why do you want to know that?"

He slid out of his chair and came to kneel beside me. He

pulled on the legs of my chair until I was facing him, my bare feet in his hands. His eyes filled with lust as his hands ran up my legs, the heat of his skin soothing down the goose bumps that had formed.

"I'm just curious is all. So, did you?"

I licked my lips as his hands kept traveling upward, stopping at my knees.

"Yes. I did. Jasmine bought us all dances."

The breath Aaron had been holding came out in a hiss. His fingers dug into my flesh, the tiny shots of pain making me crazy. Before I could say another word, he pushed my thighs apart, the tiny scrap of fabric that passed for my underwear now exposed.

"What was her name?"

"The stripper?"

"Yes, the stripper."

"Her name was Vanessa."

Aaron rubbed his thumbs along my inner thighs, each pass moving further up my legs, each stroke a delicate tease. I eased down the chair, bringing my hips forward, trying to move him along. But he did things at his own pace, just like always.

"What did she look like?"

I thought back to the girl I had seen on stage, twirling herself around the brass pole with ease. As soon as I'd seen her, I'd been transfixed. There was just something about her, something that sent a zing right to my pussy. I had no idea how I was going to explain it to Aaron, but I wanted to try.

"Blond hair, a little taller than me. Nice round hips and a great ass."

"Big tits?"

I gasped as he moved one hand up my thigh, brushing the tips of his fingers against the fabric that covered my rapidly moistening cunt. He dropped a kiss on my other leg, the warm trail of his tongue tormenting me.

"No. Not really. They just looked like they would be nice to touch. And her skin was so beautiful. Tan and smooth."

He looked up at me, his eyes on mine as I felt the crotch of my panties being pushed aside.

"Did you get a chance to touch her tits, Elisha, during the lap dance?"

I swallowed as his finger slid across my wet pussy lips, slipping between them with ease. I wanted him inside me, but he kept his distance, just the barest contact between us. I knew my next words would change all that. I couldn't wait to see his face.

"Yeah."

Aaron's mouth fell open just a bit and his free hand dropped to his crotch, his hardening cock making a tent in his flannel pajama pants.

"Shit, that's hot. Guys are never allowed to touch. You're lucky."

As his finger started to slide inside me, I kept talking.

"She did more than let me touch her. She made me."

Aaron shuddered as he started to finger-fuck me, the memories of the night flooding back. My voice was husky; the only other sound in the room was his heavy breathing.

"She was facing away from me, grinding her ass against my lap. When she leaned back, she put her hands on top of mine and slid them up her sides and over her tits. Her nipples were rock hard against my palms. After that, I couldn't resist pinching them, and she let me. In fact, she told me to do it harder. She had the sexiest voice."

"Then what happened?"

As he slowly moved his finger inside me, I pushed my hips forward again, giving him better access to my cunt. He obliged me by adding a second finger, but his pace was still slow and steady. I needed more and I knew just how to get it.

"Then she slid one of my hands down her stomach until I was touching her G-string. I thought she'd stop there, but she didn't. Before I could stop her, she pushed my hand down again and I was touching her pussy. She was so wet."

Aaron yanked me out of my chair and bent me over our kitchen table, my coffee spilling across the wood in the process. He flipped my skirt up and yanked off my thong. His hands rested on my ass, his voice nearly a growl when he spoke.

"Keep going, Elisha. I want to hear more."

I opened my mouth to speak but the words didn't come as Aaron ran his tongue down the crack of my ass, teasing my tight pucker before moving down to my wet cunt. I felt him spread me open, his tongue teasing my wet slit as his fingers slid over my clit. I pushed back against his face, inching my legs apart. Finally, I found my voice again.

"She kept moving my hand, rubbing my fingers over her clit, rolling her hips. My other hand was still on her tit, pinching her nipple. Soon, she wasn't guiding me at all. It was all me. I made her come, Aaron. Right there in the Champagne Room. It was so hot. I wish you had been there, baby. I wish you could have watched us."

He wrapped his lips around my clit and sucked hard, flicking his tongue back and forth over the sensitive bud. I cried out, my thighs starting to shake with sweet anticipation. Suddenly, his mouth was gone. He replaced it with a swift slap of his hand on my ass. Then another. And another. One more spank rained down, my skin growing hot. He leaned down over me, biting my earlobe before he spoke.

"Here I was, worried something terrible had happened to you, and you were busy fingering a stripper."

He stood back up, his hand pressed against the back of my neck, another flurry of spanks peppering my ass.

"Aaron, please. I'm sorry."

He stopped just long enough to push two fingers back inside my pussy, slicing through my wetness with ease. Three more hard slaps rang out in the room, my yells joining them. I felt tears prick the corners of my eyes, and Aaron turned me around roughly.

"Lucky for you, Elisha, I'm too horny to be mad right now."

He shoved me onto my back, my ass on the edge of the messy table. I looked up at him just in time to see him enter me and grasp one of my ankles in each hand. He pushed my legs high and wide, fucking me hard and deep.

"Play with your nipples for me, Elisha. Since you like doing it so much."

I did as he told me and exposed my breasts, rolling each nipple between a thumb and forefinger. I moaned, tightening my pussy around his hard cock, the pace of his thrusts increasing just slightly. I met his eyes; the normally warm blue looked steely cold as he fucked me, moving the table with the force of his body. He moved over me, his face inches from mine, my legs going around his back. He pressed my hands down against the table, his strength overwhelming me.

"Did Vanessa make you come, Elisha?"

I moaned as he punctuated my name with a hard stroke of his cock, my breath stolen by a rough kiss.

"No. The dance ended too fast."

"Too bad. I bet that would have been a sight to see."

The push and pull of him inside me was slowed to a crawl, my back arching as he took one of my nipples between his teeth. He released me, fucking me with abandon, rocking the whole table. I couldn't take it anymore, my body coiled tight for too long.

As his cock was in me to the hilt, I started to come, my moans swallowed by his greedy lips. Each wave knocked me over, each ebb followed by another, stronger crest. Aaron grunted right in my ear as he came. Our voices combined to make a guttural noise that echoed off the yellow walls of the kitchen.

I could barely move, even after his weight was off me. The fatigue I'd been battling all night overtook me, and I found myself scooped up in Aaron's arms and on my way to bed. As he draped the comforter over us, I nestled into the crook of his arm.

"So am I forgiven for being late, Aaron?"

"For now. But you might just need a bit more punishment later. After all, you did make me worry."

He held me tighter and gave my ass a playful slap. I sighed at the contact, my ass still tender from his slaps.

"Remind me to thank Jasmine and Ranna at the wedding."

I looked at him through barely open eyes and managed a smile. "For what?"

"For making you get a lap dance, Elisha."

"I'm sure they'll be happy to know you approve."

Aaron kissed me, the soft press of his lips stealing the last of my energy. All the coffee in the world couldn't have kept me up for much longer.

"Elisha?"

"Yes, Aaron."

"Do you think Vanessa works at the club every weekend?"

I looked at him, his mischievous smile.

"I don't know. Why?"

He planted a kiss on my forehead, pushing my hair out of my face.

"Because I thought maybe we could get her to finish that lap dance for you. And this time, I'll make sure it doesn't end too soon."

SEVEN A.M.
CHANGE
OF SHIFT

Cheyenne Blue

Andrea creeps home before daylight. The dawn is swelling outside, starting the gradual build to the day, but at the moment it's still dark inside the house. Andrea pushes the button on the coffeemaker that Kai has set ready before he went to bed the night before. As the coffee drips, she sheds her sensible nurse's shoes and releases her hair from its tight ponytail. There's no sound from the bedroom.

She steals the first cup before the coffeemaker has stopped dripping. The best cup, she calls it, the strongest and darkest, with the most flavor. She drinks it black and sweet.

The rest of the pot is ready by the time she's finished her first mug. She pours herself a refill, and a mug for Kai—milky white, no sugar. There's still no sound from the bedroom. A mug in each hand, she pads on stockinged feet to the bedroom door. The blinds are pulled down tight, but in the shadows, she can see Kai sleeping. He's sprawled on his stomach, one arm above his head. His breathing is soft and even. The sheet is down below his waist, revealing the shadowy curve of his buttocks.

Andrea watches him sleep for a moment. She wonders what time he got to bed last night. But as a junior doctor, even if it was in the small hours after a night emergency, he's still expected to be dressed in a clean white coat, trailing behind the consultant, nodding sagely as the consultant does the early-morning rounds.

She's turning, starting to creep away to let him sleep that bit longer, when he stirs, rolls over, stretches, and says, "Busy night?"

He sounds wide awake, as if he's only been feigning sleep, but Andrea knows that's not the case. He's used to being jolted awake for medical emergencies; he knows how to leap into consciousness in an instant.

"Not too bad. Only a couple of cases. And Bibi brought gumbo, so we ate well."

He nods. He understands the jerky pace of the operating room at night: adrenaline, and hasty bites of tepid cafeteria leftovers when it's busy; chatter, catnaps, and reheated home-cooked food when it's quiet. He glances at the clock and Andrea says, "You can sleep for another hour if you want."

"No." He moves to one side of the bed. "Join me?"

"I need a shower first."

"Later. After I've left." He flips the sheet back and reveals his erection, large and luscious, lying flat against his belly.

Kai's morning erections are indeed a thing of wonder. Kai is far from her first lover, but his cock is impressive, even by Andrea's standards. It's as if his arousal is tied to the dawn, running in sync with the building of the day. She's watched him before, and as dawn's fingers creep through the cracks in the blinds, as darkness segues to gray morning, Kai swells along with the light.

Andrea's and Kai's body clocks are out of sync most of the time—a nurse's night duty and a junior doctor's erratic hours see to that—but mornings are when it comes together for them.

She wrinkles her nose. "I smell of antiseptic." She hands him the mug of coffee. "Drink this while I shower."

As she sheds her clothes, he's already propped against the pillows, inhaling steam.

She pads back naked and smelling of citrus and toothpaste to find he's opened the blinds. The sun cracks over the horizon, and as the daylight builds, so does Kai's energy. She, on the other hand, is falling toward sleep.

He flings back the quilt and she crawls in next to him, aligning her body to his. He's golden skinned, warm brown like fall foliage, in the growing light in the bedroom; she's pale as milk. Neither of them get much sun—their skins are their own natural color. The contrast is only one of the things she loves about him, about them together. Andrea rests her head on his smooth chest. His skin is smoother than her own, and she often teases him that he waxes, tweezes, shaves, all the things that society says she ought to do but seldom does. Hospital scrubs hide many things, including body hair. But Kai doesn't mind: indeed, he loves her fuzzy forearms, the stray dark hairs around her nipples, and the jungly luxuriant bush that makes bikini wearing impossible.

Andrea sighs a deep breath and considers sleep. But Kai is already running his hand along her arm, his fingers making exploratory forays onto the curve of her breast as it rests on his chest. He hums deep in his throat, a strange rumble of apprecia-tion that she hears underneath her ear on his chest.

His hands lift away the tiredness, and she lets him build a response in her until she's awake and aroused and the post-work lethargy dissipates into something that buzzes and flickers with an overlay of energy.

Sex for Andrea and Kai is seldom a long, drawn-out symphony of sighs and slow crescendos. Their work is immediate, a life lived on the edge of reaction, and they've learned to live with that urgency. Meals are often gulped standing up at the breakfast bar. There are no long debates about where to go for a beer. One will suggest, the other agree, and they're out of the door within five minutes of the decision. Their working lives are patterned with interruptions and necessary changes of focus, and that has spilled over into their time together. Besides, there's the ever-present pager, which can summon most often Kai, less often Andrea, back to the Great God Hospital which rules their lives. Long and slow doesn't do it for them; fast and furious does.

So now, her interest assured, Kai rolls Andrea onto her back and kisses her. Kisses her as if he's drowning and only her breath can save him; deep, hot, wet kisses. His tongue explores her mouth, advancing and retreating, much as his cock presses and relaxes against her leg. He tastes of coffee and impatience.

She rises to his kiss, her hands skimming his golden body, over the muscles that are firm from youth alone since he has no time for exercise, grasping his lean buttocks and grinding her thigh against his cock. She's fully with him now, diving into the urgency, her body already shimmering toward crescendo. She grasps his head and arches her back, directing his attention down to her nipples. Kai complies, his cock leaving a damp smear on her thigh as he moves down her body.

He suckles with a ferocity that takes her to the edge of pain, his teeth lightly scraping over skin and nipple. She pushes her breast into his mouth as he works her nipple into such a point of pleasure that each suck sends an impulse to her clit as intense as if he'd touched his mouth to her breast. Andrea is full-breasted, and Kai laves the skin, his breath eager and hot as he kisses her nipple, bites gently on its surrounds, then hard enough to leave a mark. His fingers reach for her other breast, and he rolls her nipple with dexterous surgeon's fingers.

For long moments she falls into the joy of pure sensation, reveling in her lover's touch. But her mind is already moving on to the next level, and her body is following fast. Andrea pushes his shoulder, urging him away from her breast. She wants his cock, wants to feel the satin skin move under her fingers. Kai rolls onto his back. Andrea strums her fingers up his length and bends to touch him with her lips. Her tongue swirls around his tip, laps his salty taste, while he raises his hips to meet her mouth.

Andrea swings around, settles her knees either side of his head and lowers her body within reach of his tongue. For long moments, there are only lips and tongues and pleasure, and the dampness of skin, the moistness of cock and cunt. Andrea used to be self-conscious about this, too concerned about what her lovers would see, what they would smell to fully relax into the sensation, but over time, and an appreciation of her own body, that worry passed, and now she delights in the sensation. Kai loves doing this to her; he says often that he would stay between her thighs for the morning, if only responsibility would allow.

She's attuned to his lips on her pussy. Each pass of his tongue over her clit, each hot damp exhalation, each slide of a finger inside her pussy spirals her closer to the edge. His mouth is already pushing her toward climax; the flicker on her clit builds sensation faster than any vibrator. She's learned not to delay but to embrace the swell—the Great God Hospital has robbed her of orgasms in the past. And then, if there's time, there'll be another.

So she clenches her belly, closes her eyes, and her mouth goes slack on Kai's shaft. His tongue pries her open, dips inside and then circles her clit until she comes hard in shudders of pleasure, her thighs tightening on his ears.

She relaxes, inhales deeply and closes her eyes for a moment. When she opens them, his cock is still hard and proud in front of her. Andrea presses her lips to the tip, laps the salty fluid, then takes him deep. For a moment, she's tempted to return the favor, to suck him until he floods her mouth with his fluid, but Kai twines his hand in her hair and urges her up. She sits up, shuffles down his body, then moves off him. She can see his face now, he's smiling, and she can see his cock: erect, veined and pulsating. The sleep that she'd pushed aside for sex overwhelms her for a moment, and in her post-orgasmic haze she wants nothing more than to lie down and let it claim her. But Kai is waiting, his energy growing. It's as if he's taking her remaining energy to push her toward sleep and she lets him, helping him toward the day.

She rolls onto her back, raising one knee in invitation. Andrea knows the missionary position is unoriginal, but she loves it anyway. She loves the feel of him cradled in her thighs, loves how they can kiss as they fuck, loves the full body contact and how deep he can push inside her.

She loves it most at this time of morning, when she's falling toward sleep. Then she lets Kai do most of the work and she can close her eyes and drift on a sexual sea of somnolence, let him advance and withdraw like the tide.

Kai moves on top and pushes inside with one blunt thrust. He sets a relentless rhythm, a fast fucking, a winter storm of a tide rather than a lazy summer one. Andrea closes her eyes, lets him pound away on top of her and lets him set the surge and retreat. Only her inner muscles clench and relax; the rest of her is boneless and soft.

"Andrea," he says, and bites her neck, rousing her from lethargy.

She obliges, opens her eyes and drowns deep in his dark ones. She grasps his buttocks, starts moving with the rhythm. She won't come again, she knows that already, but she loves it like this as she can watch Kai take his pleasure.

He rises above her so that the cool air touches their bodies in contrast to the heated point of their joining.

She urges him on with voice and fingers, for delay is a dangerous thing in the mornings when one of them is on duty. But he swells within her, and hesitates, easing the pounding beat to a softer, subtler, more gradual slide. He's close, she knows, close enough that he must be poised on the edge of orgasm, close enough that he can finish in an instant.

He smiles down at her, kisses her mouth, pushes back her hair with tenderness. She turns her head and catches his fingers as they glide past. He's barely moving within her, still hard, still swollen, but only the barest friction as he teeters on the brink.

And his beeper goes, shrilling into the stillness, a discordant blast of sound. The Great God Hospital calls and he must obey.

The noise rouses him, and instantly he's pumping hard and fast, and his face is no longer soft and tender. His head is thrown back, his eyes closed as he focuses on his climax and how quickly he can get there. One thrust, two, three, and before the pager has stopped he's started and he pulsates his heat deep inside her.

In the single beat of stillness of afterward, they lie still joined. Kai rests his forehead against Andrea's and kisses her, the briefest of pecks. A moment of silence before the cacophony that is his day. Then he withdraws, his cock leaving a sticky trail across her leg, and he's out of bed, fumbling for the pager, reading the message.

Andrea lies and watches him, handing him the phone so he can call the hospital.

"Yes, yes..." he says. "Crossmatch three units of blood. I'll be there in fifteen minutes."

The shower splashes on, and he's in and out in under three minutes. Jeans, a crumpled shirt, stethoscope already around his neck, clean white coat over arm.

He rests a knee on the bed and bends to kiss her. "I hope I'll see you before you leave for work this evening," he says. His lips are warm and taste of distraction. "Love you, Andi."

He's gone, fumbling for car keys, stepping into his shoes at the front door, which slams behind him.

Andrea remains in bed, her body already drifting toward sleep. She knows she should wipe Kai's spend from her thighs before it stains the sheets. She should pee, and she should brush her teeth. She does none of these things. At this changeover of the day, the juncture between so many things—light and dark, night and day, awake and asleep, her ending and Kai's beginning—she just wants to lie and let her mind unravel.

Andrea sleeps.

EIGHT A.M. MORNING WOOD

Georgia E. Jones

Adam was grumpy in the morning.

Adam was grumpy every morning. He was not a morning person. He got home from tending bar around three a.m., knocked around the house until four or four-thirty and woke up grumpy sometime before noon. On the good side of this, he was fine by the time I came home from work, and a light sleeper he was not. I could stage a reenactment of Antietam in the bedroom and he could sleep right through it. Me, on the other hand? I woke up wanting sex. The average guy with morning wood had nothing on me. Sometimes I woke with a jolt, falling back into my body from a dream of having someone inside me and all I wanted was to roll over, suck Adam until he was hard, then mount his cock and ride him until I came. Inadvisable. The one time I tried resulted in our first (and only, to be fair) bad fight. Adam didn't want to be woken up in the morning—not even for hot, sweaty, happy sex.

I woke at my usual time and climbed out of bed, having no

good reason to stay in it, with only one regretful, backwards glance. I padded around the room naked, picking up my clothes from the day before. I brushed my teeth. I looked for the missing turquoise earring and found it, much to my delight, under the blue chair. Backing out from beneath it, I saw Adam had one eye open and one closed. Creepy. Was he asleep with one eye open or awake with one eye closed? I knew better than to ask. I turned my back on him and sauntered over to the dresser. If he was awake, the open eye would have a nice view of my ass, which he liked. I put the earring back on the stand with its mate, then ran my hand down the slope of my breast and pinched my nipple until it was stiff and pebbly between my fingers. Then I gave the other one the same treatment. I propped one foot on the open bottom drawer of the dresser and turned my knee out so I could reach my clit. I stroked it, thinking of Adam's body, his cock, his lips. "What're you doing?" he asked. His voice was gravelly-low-rough-delicious.

I flicked him a quick glance over my shoulder, my fingers still moving. "Nothing," I said calmly. "Didn't mean to wake you." This state of affairs went on for a few minutes. I touched myself until I was wet. I brought my hand up and slicked moisture over my nipples and sucked it off my fingers. I readjusted the angle of my foot on the drawer, opening myself wider. There was no sound from behind me. Asleep, then. I sighed, minding less. I was prepared to come right there, though I had never done it like that before in front of Adam. Though, since he was asleep, I wasn't sure what I was doing counted as "in front of."

"C'mere," he said.

I turned. He was awake, watching me with sleepy, heavy-lidded eyes, sprawled out naked and loose-limbed, the sheet riding low on his hips. My eyes followed the line of his torso, the smattering of black hair trailing down his belly. He had a habit of making orders sound sweet. Any other man would have ended up with his shoe up his ass, but Adam said things to me— get down on your knees, put your mouth on my cock—and I complied without arguing. I saw him. Part of his fierceness was bravado. He didn't want to be messed with, so he messed first. But as soon as he realized he was being dealt with in good faith, he gave the same in return.

He stretched, languorous, and I could see the bulge of his cock under the sheet. "Come here, little girl," he said again. "I'm going to help you out." He was twenty-nine...and I wasn't. But he called me that, sometimes, and I liked it. I walked to the bed and looked down at him, the slanted cat eyes and bristly mustache. He pulled the sheet back. "This is how this is going to work: you climb on and do something that makes you happy and I'll lie here with my eyes closed. I might be awake."

I was gone on him, because I thought this was a sterling offer. He wasn't kidding. His eyes were closed again. But his cock was engorged, pulsing with heat. I straddled him, his solid thighs taking my weight easily. I went slowly. I sank the tip of his cock inside me and leaned forward, hands braced on his broad chest, moving just enough to keep him there. His cock was long—long enough to rub my G-spot when we fucked— and it was wide, so wide I felt stretched and invaded when he was inside me. I took more of him, making breathy noises of pleasure. His eyes were still closed, but I thought I detected a slight tensing of the muscles below me. Tired of playing, I sat up, groaning a little as I took all of him inside me. I rocked against him, rubbing my clit on the smooth soft skin right above his cock, which he shaved for me. I was being noisier now, closer to coming, my inner muscles beginning to clench around him.

His hands clamped over my hips. "Make it last," he said.

My eyes flew open, accusing. "You're supposed to be asleep!"
He arched a brow. "Really? I'm not. Slow down."

"No!" I actually argued with him, sitting on his cock, wriggling my clit against him. "You said I could please myself," I reminded him desperately.

"You have," he said, lifting me and bringing me back down, thrusting strongly into me at the same time. My head went back and I shut up. He moved me where he wanted me, that big cock relentless inside me, and he kept me higher up so my clit couldn't rub against him. Soon every breath was a gasp. I leaned forward and bit him, not tenderly, at the juncture of his neck and shoulder. "No biting," he said, but I could tell from his voice that he liked it.

"Let me come," I begged, shameless. "Let me come or I'll bite."

"No," he said. I didn't know if that was no, don't bite me, or no, don't come, and it hardly mattered, because in the next instant he rolled me under him, pushing my thighs as wide as they would go, hammering into me. He let my hips go and brought his finger to bear on my aching clit—sweet man, I would forgive him anything—and kept it there until I splintered with a keening sound. He came, too, almost as an afterthought, and held me until I quieted down.

I kissed his lax mouth. "Thank you," I whispered. "Go back to sleep now." But he already was.

NINE A.M.
OFFICE
BRIEFING

Justine Elyot

She stops at the watercooler to unparch her throat.

"Hey, good weekend, Ms. Forrester?"

"Really good, thanks. You?"

Raymond Bland is clearly about to embark on a blow-by-blow account of his Sunday League football match, so she holds up a hand, gulping down the water before apologizing.

"Sorry, can't stop. I've got a briefing with Stanshaw at nine."

"Oh, sure, you wouldn't want to be late for that."

He makes a comedy cutthroat gesture.

Alisha laughs, an all-pals-together oh-god-I-know kind of laugh.

Then she feels disloyal.

Then she puts a hand to her thigh and rubs her skirt, checking that the suspender snaps haven't come undone.

Because that would never do.

Raymond saunters off to high-five one of the IT technicians

and Alisha takes a moment to breathe. This might be the last uninterrupted breath she gets until the briefing is over, after all.

Stanshaw's office door is shut but presumably he is in there. He is always an hour early for work.

"Can you let him know I'm here, Jo?" she asks his secretary.

There is no sign of excessive curiosity or sneery knowingness in Jo's brief phone message, but Alisha still can't help thinking that she knows. Does she know? Could she?

Alisha opens the office door and breathes in the scent of polished wood and luxury carpeting, aromas that always now arouse her.

The minute hand on the clock opposite the desk clicks up to point directly at the twelve.

Success.

"Well done," says Stanshaw, taking off his spectacles to polish them without dropping his gaze from Alisha's face. "Perfect timing."

He has not invited her to sit down, so she stands by the door, hands clasped over her skirt.

"Shall we start with a kit inspection?"

He rises to his feet and she pushes back her shoulders and raises her chin unthinkingly, dropping her arms to her sides.

"Nice posture," he says, drawing closer until his height advantage over her is obvious and inescapable. "Take off your jacket."

She unbuttons carefully, eases it down her arms.

He takes it from her and hangs it up.

"Shoulders right back," he reminds her softly. "Thrust out those breasts—as far as you can. Good. Now, let's have that shirt off."

She is grateful to him for turning the heating up a notch.

All the same, her nipples stiffen once they lose the protective layer of businesslike cotton. Already hard with excitement, they tighten into painful knots.

Stanshaw's finger traces the line of her bra cups, down one, up the other.

"Pretty," he says. "Now. Skirt."

She reaches behind and unzips. The knee-length silk-lined wool slides coolly over her thighs, then pools around her feet.

"Ah, well done. You got my email, then."

"Yes, Sir."

The directive about knickers being forbidden during office hours this week. Yes, she'd opened that one after breakfast on Sunday morning. The washing-up had had to wait until she'd dealt with the itch the email had provoked.

"Turn around."

She rotates slowly, giving him a slow reveal of her naked bottom, then turns back around to display her suspender-framed shaved pussy and golden upper thighs.

"Did you buy those especially for me?"

"Yes, Sir."

Her first stockings, bought along with the suspender belt on Saturday afternoon in a luxury department store. She had felt excited and wicked and embarrassed handing the items over to the cashier, fumbling with her purse and avoiding her eye. She could only be buying them for sex. That was their sole reason for existing.

"Yes," she imagined herself blurting, "yes, I am going to get fucked. Want to make something of it?"

And now they cling to her skin, covering it while exposing it.

Stanshaw's finger burrows inside one of the straps and strokes up and down, rough knuckle dragging against smooth flesh.

"Yes, you'll do," he says. "Now, I suppose we should move

on to the briefing proper. I'll take your report over my desk, Ms. Forrester."

She knows what he means by that.

"Oh, you need to take the bra off first, of course." He catches himself, stunned at his omission.

Alisha frees her breasts, then shudders at the thought of pressing those poor bare mounds down on to the cold, hard walnut desk.

But it has to be done.

She reaches across to the far side, not quite able to grip the opposite edge because the desk is vast. Instead, her palms lie flat on the leather blotter while her nipples squash into the varnish.

She has worn her highest heels, all the better to present her arse to his view.

One of his hands cups the curve, just holding it there, more a promise than a caress. Or should she say, a threat?

"Let's have those figures, Ms. Forrester," he says.

She takes a deep breath, holds it at the top of her lungs, steadying herself.

"Industrial action on public transport impacted a number of offices, resulting in a higher than usual level of staff absence, especially at the Newbridge and Holkham Wood branches. Therefore, productivity was not as high as it was last week. Sickness absence remains static at two percent, excluding staff with long-term medical problems. One machine broke down and needed costly replacement parts, but seven clients settled accounts. However, overall, profit for the week fell by..."

She grits her teeth. She knows he's going to love this.

"Three hundred and seventy-two pounds."

"Three hundred and seventy-two? Are you sure?"

"Positive. I triple-checked the figures."

"Well, that's unprecedented. Our worst week since I started here."

"I know, Sir. The strike action couldn't be helped..."

"No, but all the same..."

Silence falls. Alisha barely dares to breathe. Breath will only interfere with her attempts to gauge his mood and her fate.

"Well, I don't see the benefit of sparing the rod," he says at last. "This can't be repeated, and the message needs to be clear and unequivocal. So it's going to be five minutes with my hand, followed by twenty with the strap, then six with the cane to finish off."

She bites her lip, determined not to whine. But this is her hardest penalty yet. She knows that strap of old, and it is both heavy and cruel. Not as cruel as the cane, though, which is her most feared of implements.

He starts with his hand, easy at first, pacing himself. It's in nobody's interest to take Alisha beyond her levels of endurance. The smack-smack-smack reverberates around the office. He's said before that it's well soundproofed, but Alisha can never quite dismiss that element of doubt, thinking of Jo at her desk outside.

She keeps hold of her self-control, breathing evenly, making it a matter of pride not to cry out or kick or flail. Her bottom warms, slowly but relentlessly, the tingle graduating to a smart.

"It won't do, will it, Ms. Forrester?" says Stanshaw, spanking on and on. "Too many weeks like that and we'll all be out of a job, won't we?"

"Yes, Sir."

"It's all very well to blame forces beyond our control, but we can still make plans and preparations. We can organize car shares. We can put agency staff on standby. Can't we?"

"Yes, Sir." She begins to struggle with her composure. She

wants to protest, *But there wasn't enough notice!* As if excuses will make a shred of difference.

He pushes an open manual under her nose.

"Read the top paragraph," he instructs with a smack of reinforcement.

She spends the remainder of her hand-spanking sentence reading haltingly from the section on effective management while Stanshaw's palm falls repeatedly on her suffering bum.

While he plies the strap, she has to read from her job description, but now it is not possible to let the sentences flow smoothly. They are interrupted by gasps and whimpers until eventually she is only able to utter a few broken syllables between strokes.

Her legs begin to tremble, even though most of her weight is supported by the desk. She thinks about using her safeword, but his arm comes to rest and she realizes that the twenty strokes have been dealt.

"Taking the cane isn't going to be easy today," he says gently, fingertips grazing her heated flesh.

"It never is, Sir." Her voice wobbles but she feels she owes it to him to demonstrate some resilience of spirit. He mustn't think he's broken her.

"No, no, I suppose not. But it must be done. Lessons must be learned, Ms. Forrester. After all, if you fail in your position, then we all run the risk of losing ours. Don't we?"

"I suppose so, Sir."

He has her count the six cane strokes and thank him for each one. He takes his time, giving her plenty of time to anticipate and dread each falling cut, choosing each target with care.

He stripes her behind perfectly; five parallel welts, crossed fiendishly with the final diagonal stroke. His mark upon her, ensuring that she will be avoiding sitting down for the rest of the day.

Her head on the desk is spinning. The fire behind takes up every scrap of her attention; the rest of her body might as well have fallen apart. She feels she could stay there all day, sinking into the wood, eventually merging with it.

But Stanshaw has other plans. He follows each welt with a fingertip, keeping the pain fresh, then bends to kiss them.

"It's been too long since I caned you," he whispers. "And how about here...oh...yes. So wet."

Alisha's hips wriggle at the sudden contact of finger and clit. Stanshaw massages her pussy, dipping deep, drawing from her well. Despite the unceasing sting—or because of it—she sighs and pushes back for more.

"Later," he says with a chuckle. "You have to give me your official thanks."

She needs a few moments but eventually she is able to haul herself to her feet, turn around and drop to her knees.

Without a word, she takes Stanshaw's hard cock from his suit trousers and lowers her mouth onto it.

There is something about having a sore bottom that makes her relish this task and give it every ounce of her lascivious strength. The heat spurs her on, makes her throat deeper, her tongue faster, her suck stronger. She cups his balls eagerly, devouring his prick as if her life depends on it.

When he fills her mouth she swallows it greedily, licking every last drop from his shaft before withdrawing with a final loving lick and raising her eyes, like a faithful dog with the stick it's retrieved from a bush.

She watches his chest rise and fall, watches the vivid color begin to drain from his cheeks, watches his eyes de-glaze.

"All right," he says. "Lotion. Back over the desk."

Now her reward comes, in the form of cold cream melting into those buzzing stripes. Sensitive fingers dance across the stinging skin, then they move lower, lower still, until they delve between her pussy lips, ready to give her something to be really grateful for.

"I'm going to let you come this time," he says, dealing ruthlessly with her clit. "I did question whether you deserved it...but you took the whipping well, and I guess you do need a little bit of positive motivation. After all, we can't have our managing director feeling too down in the dumps, can we?"

"No, Sir. Ooh. Oh, that's good."

One hand busies itself with Alisha's clit while the other digs inside her, thrusting two fingers, then three, up her soaked and spasming cunt. She writhes vigorously on the desk, feeling her orgasm approach from afar, a tiny seed growing and blooming in the pit of her stomach.

"A happy boss...happy staff...happy workplace...motivation and profit." He intones catchphrases and buzzwords while Alisha begins to slap the desk, humping Stanshaw's fingers for all she is worth.

"You need to come, don't you? You always need to come after a spanking. What does that make you, hmm?"

"Bad, oh, a bad girl, oh."

She comes, jolting and banging the desk, while he spears her with deadly efficiency, holding his fingers inside until she flops in a lifeless heap.

She lies there for a while, her breath misting up the walnut sheen of the desk, then she peels herself off it and turns to face Stanshaw, who is in the corner fussing with the cafetière.

"Could you pass me my skirt?"

He hands it over with a smile and watches her dress once the coffees are poured.

"Should be a bit better this week," he remarks.

"Oh yes, I should think so. Your branch was one of the few

that held their own last week, actually. I think your carpooling system saved the day there."

"Thanks. Perhaps it could be a company-wide policy?"

"I'll certainly mention it to the board tonight. We have the Christmas bonuses to consider as well."

She finishes buttoning her jacket and takes the coffee cup.

"Ah. The Christmas bonus. That's how all this started, of course. Do you remember?"

She could hardly forget. Alisha allows her memory to drift back to that late-November afternoon visit to Stanshaw's branch. Ever since he'd taken over at the helm there, she'd found her flirtation with him becoming more and more ungovernable. It was crazy—the managing director and her lowly vassal—but she couldn't seem to help herself.

"We're considering introducing a Christmas bonus scheme," she'd said, once they were face-to-face in the big comfortable office.

"Christmas…?" He pretended to mishear, smirking.

"I said bonus, not boner, Mr. Stanshaw! Don't look at me like that."

"Sorry, got a little overexcited. Take it from my salary."

"Oh, I wouldn't take anything from you. Except maybe…"

"Go on!"

"No, I can't."

"Tell me."

"Oh, that sounded really masterful! Say it again."

He growled this time. "Tell me."

"What will you do to me if I don't?"

The delirious feeling of crossing the line goaded them both onward, into an uncharted terrain of unprofessionalism. But neither could stop, and neither wanted to. That afternoon, Stanshaw's Christmas bonus had been bestowed in the form of hot sex over the desk. Alisha had left the office with laddered tights and disordered hair. If Jo noticed, she didn't mention it. But of course, she wouldn't.

And now here they are locked into this curious sub-dom relationship, carried out on a fortnightly basis.

Alisha opts to stand up to drink her coffee.

Stanshaw is about to say something about the Christmas bonus, but his phone rings. He picks it up with an apologetic grimace.

"Yes. Sorry. Yes, I know. We've been thrashing out the figures. I'll be another fifteen, maybe twenty minutes. Bye."

Alisha, who has snorted a bit of coffee through her nose at the phrase *thrashing out the figures*, dabs at her jacket with her handkerchief.

"Yes," says Stanshaw, resuming after the interruption. "It's our anniversary, of sorts, isn't it? We should celebrate."

"I think we already did."

"No, I mean...ah, well. You know. Sometimes I think it'd be nice..."

He trails off, making Alisha feel obscurely guilty.

"You want to...you know...outside the office?"

He shakes his head, his eyes occluded.

"I feel like a sex object sometimes," he says eventually.

"Oh! Luke, I had no idea. I thought this arrangement, well, I thought you were happy with it."

"I know you're a busy woman, but would you ever consider...?"

She already has. But the inequality between them has always prevented her making any kind of move.

She leans back against a filing cabinet, making sure her tender bottom doesn't bump up against the unforgiving metal. It feels so delicious, this literal afterglow. The man who gives

it to her does have a special place in her heart, if only he could
know it.

"Tell you what, Luke," she says softly, her hand not so steady
under the saucer now. "It's the Christmas do on Friday. Do you
want to take me?"

"I always want to take you."

"Then I'll pick you up at six-thirty. Now, are we briefed?"

"I'd say so."

"So would I. Thanks for the coffee."

She walks past Jo, acknowledging her with a brisk nod and
a tight smile.

The workers at the watercooler are clearly discussing her,
gossiping about her private life.

Well, why not give them something to gossip about? Forrester
Industries is strong enough to take it, after all.

TEN A.M. KICKOFF

Donna George Storey

I never really got the appeal of football until I met Alex. Why would I? I grew up in a family of three sisters who all favored ballet over team sports. Sometimes my father would watch a play-off game in the family room, but it all seemed so mysterious. No matter how often Dad explained the rules, I could never figure out why the "down" kept changing from first to second then back to first again. Eventually I gave up trying. Football was for boys anyway.

I met Alex in June, at a party. By August I was practically living at his place. He didn't have a roommate, so it was much easier to spend whole weekends in bed, getting up only to refuel with takeout or gelato, before we went at it again.

Then one Sunday morning in early September, Alex did not immediately reach for me as soon as he opened his eyes. Instead he reached for the remote and turned on the East Coast football game.

The honeymoon was obviously over.

I lay beside him pretending to sleep while I nursed my broken heart. Still, Alex looked so handsome as he watched the game, propped against two pillows, his hands behind his head, an easy smile on his face. Not that he was exactly relaxed. I could feel his body stiffen and quiver with each exciting play, a tension that found release in a spirited howl when things went wrong for his team and a hearty cheer when things went right. Both sounded raw and unmistakably erotic to me.

After the first quarter, I had to admit I was getting very turned on. As in stiff nipples, tingly belly, joy juice wetting my thighs. I considered masturbating for relief—maybe he'd be so caught up in the action on TV he wouldn't even notice?—but somehow that felt like admitting defeat before the game was over.

So I snuggled up against him, sliding my leg over his so that my crotch was pressed against his muscular thigh.

He grunted agreeably and patted my head.

The announcer's voice rose in excitement. Alex's body tensed again. He let out a sigh of victory and relaxed into the mattress. I used that as an excuse to rock my hips forward, grinding my clit against his leg.

Alex glanced down at me with a faint frown. He had to be aware how aroused I was. I could feel my slickness as my pussy skated up and down over his skin.

His hand crept toward me, and I thought, for a stomach-churning moment, that he was going to push me away. Instead he brushed my nipple through my nightshirt, then took the stiff tip between his fingers and tweaked it.

A jolt of electric pleasure shot straight to my groin. I moaned aloud into his shoulder.

He laughed softly. Then let me languish there, unattended, while he swore at the ref's bad call.

A few moments later, he was back to me. "You're humping

me just like a little dog in heat," he whispered in his "dirty" sex voice.

I gasped at the lewd words and rubbed against him some more.

"First down! Yesss!"

How the hell was I going to keep his attention on me instead of that damn game? Desperate for an ally, I curled my fingers around his hard cock. It twitched in solidarity.

Alex looked down at me again, as if deciding what to do. Then he did push me away, rearranging our bodies so I was on my back and he was on his side. One hand slipped around my shoulders to caress my breast, the other cupped my mons. Caught in his embrace, I'd lost my power to control my own stimulation. His cock, too, was safe from the temptations of my wandering hands.

"You be a good girl until halftime," he warned, his eyes still fixed on the TV screen.

I whimpered in protest, but could do little but surrender to my fate.

Which wasn't as bad as it seemed at first. Alex didn't ignore me completely. He doled out bits of pleasure between plays like single kernels of buttered popcorn. A palm circling over a nipple here, an idle stroking of my slit there. Just enough to get me arching up and breathing fast. Gradually we established little rituals of celebration. A first down for his team earned my breasts a few hot kisses. A touchdown won me a spirited clit strumming that brought me almost to the verge—before his fingers retreated to the remote to check the game on the other channel.

After a while, my lust hovered at a steady simmer even through the breaks. Yet each new ministration raised the temperature a few degrees until my flesh seemed to melt into a puddle of pussy juice beneath my ass.

At long last, halftime arrived.

Alex turned to me with smoldering eyes. Apparently he'd been simmering, too. He straddled me and spread my thighs with his knees, a male trick that makes me feel utterly and deliciously dominated. I arched up to take him in, but he taunted me one last time, that hard, red cock pointed straight at my hungry hole.

"Time for a little penetration into the end zone?" The words were clever, but his voice was thick with desire.

I jerked my pelvis up and he slipped right in. My walls were so exquisitely swollen, the sweet pressure sent a shock through my body.

Alex bent forward and took my nipple between his lips. He knew I liked it rougher when I was this turned on, and he sucked hard. I could tell he was still holding back, but I was through with waiting. I was the one to thrust up against him, the headboard beating quick time against the wall. First down, second down, third down, touchdown, that's when I came, the pulsing in my belly exploding in a series of shattering contractions. The first spasm lasted an eternity, and I let out a wail of release. Alex began to pump into me, and the headboard resumed its knocking, steady at first, then crazier and wilder until he roared out his pleasure. I swear I could feel his cock shudder as he filled me with his cream.

I had no idea a spectator sport could give you such a workout.

Alex looked deep into my eyes and smiled. "Ready for the second half?"

So now you know how I became a football fan. And why September can't come soon enough for me.

ELEVEN A.M.
ELEVENSES

Jeremy Edwards

First, the glass of iced coffee—in the kitchen, while they went through the mail—then a shower, and then terry robes in that odd alcove off the bedroom, which even the Realtor couldn't tell them much about. (Sewing room—with no windows? Walk-in closet—when the bedroom itself already had a bigger one?) Cilla and Drew had thrown a boom box in there and used the alcove daily as a private chill-out lounge, for post-shower quality time. It was one of their little routines.

"Wait a sec. I need to put something in the boom box."

"Uh-uh, Drew. You need to put something in *my* boom box. Get your cute terry-cloth ass over here."

"That's funny—I see a cute terry-cloth ass, all right... but it's not on me. See? It's right *here*."

"Hee-hee! Slap it again. Again!"

Cilla hadn't realized how much she was a creature of routine until all their routines were put in storage.

Oh, it was for a good reason. A positive reason, even. A

happy reason, in theory. She and Drew were moving to California because her dream job had become a reality. Leaving the
wintry climes of the upper Midwest behind them was no hard-
ship, either.

There was no question that it was totally worth it. She was
heading west with the most cherished thing she had—Drew—
and all the sacrifices were, she had to admit, miniscule ones.
Giving up their daily routine of looking out at the lake over
breakfast, for example. Or their routine of taking an evening
walk, in all but the fiercest weather, past the hardware store and
Russian deli and dry cleaner's.

The routine of showering in tandem, steamy buttocks
squeezed against wet pubic fur, in a quirky, narrow shower stall
that they could just manage to make work as a twosome—a
deliciously tight fit.

Sitting dazed in the cab of a rented truck while they logged
mile after mile in the middle of nowhere, Cilla told herself that
there would be new breakfast routines, new walks to explore, a
new shower...maybe even a new alcove to fuck in.

"Mmm, hee-hee. That's more like it. What's your opinion of
my *alcove?*"

"Ooh. Very comfy."

"Don't be shy, now: come *all* the way in, and I'll warm you
up. Ahhhhh, yeah, like that."

But all she could feel right now was the disorientation of
being afloat in a routineless sea. *Was this what it felt like for
astronauts to be in zero-g?* she wondered.

It didn't seem to bother Drew. This didn't surprise Cilla;
after all, Cilla had been surprised to find that it bothered *her.*
And Drew, of course, could tell how much it bothered her, with
a minimum of explanation. When you were alone in the cab
of a U-Haul for twelve hours a day with your life partner, few

emotional nuances went unnoticed.

She gave herself another eyeful of flat road and barren landscape and utterly bored-looking sky. It boggled the mind how a vehicle could go so fast and still take this long to get to the next chunk of nothingness.

At least living motel to motel brought the perk of motel *sex*. The cold beer and warm fuck that beckoned at the end of each interstate installment gave her something to look forward to each day—and something pleasant to consider over the course of the following day.

So today, in between mourning lost routines, she was savoring last night's memory of sitting on the edge of the bed with her panties at her knees and her cunt lips glistening while Drew finished washing up. She'd been so horny she didn't want to wait for him to pull her underwear down.

She'd stood to greet him when he exited the bathroom, and within seconds she was turned 180 and laughing sensuously as he urged his cock against the softness of her naked derrière, steering her gently by the elbows to guide her back toward the bed—leading her in a dance she always called "ass rhapsody" in her mind because it made her cheeks tingle all over as if with a thousand miniature orgasms.

It made them tingle anew to think of it now.

She wondered if she should check herself before she got too deep into this reminiscence. After all, if she lingered too long on the scenario, she'd end up with a hand down her pants and the irresistible come-on of damp panties snarled in her groove. She'd be shifting in place to make them scrape against her clit, twisting her hips just so, again and again, and she'd—oh—she'd…right there in the passenger seat, in broad daylight, she'd—

"Ohhhhhh."

"What's on your mind?" Driver Drew couldn't resist teasing

her the moment her little climax had dissipated. She still had her fingers wedged firmly into her jeans.

She teased back by playing dumb. "On my mind? Nothing. Why do you ask?"

"Well, I was wondering if perchance you were engaged in a sexual fantasy, given the whole hand-down-your-jeans thing. Then that little 'Ohhhhhh'"—here he did a fair impression of her mini-orgasm—"kind of clinched it. Er...*cinched* it?"

"Either." She knew because she'd had to look this up while composing a memo the other day.

"Okay, then. It cinched it and clinched it." He glanced down at her thighs, which were pulsing together and apart, together and apart, around the shape of her buried hand. "Then again, maybe I mean *clenched* it."

It was strange as hell to feel herself convulsing with what she'd thought was going to be laughter but ended up being a spontaneous outburst of crying as another wave of homesickness overpowered her.

"Hey," Drew said tenderly, "what's wrong?"

"I don't get it," she confessed between sobs. "I'm thrilled about what we're doing, and I know we'll only be on the road a few more days. I guess I just have a silly attachment to all the special ways we did things at home. I"—she sobbed again—"I miss every tiny detail of how we arranged our life."

"It's not silly," he replied calmly, soothingly. "I think it's completely normal. If anything, I think maybe *I'm* the weird one, for not being more affected by moving. Sure, people move across the country every day of the year, and we all take that for granted. But it's a hell of a big transition, after a decade in one place. You and I put down roots back there. And it's all those tiny details that reveal it."

"You really understand." He usually did. Cilla caught her

breath and told herself to be patient with her emotional turbulence. Drew was right: it *wasn't* silly, and that thought was comforting in itself.

Five minutes later, she saw him bump the turn signal up with the knuckles of his right hand—a method that Cilla could never reproduce, which she consequently viewed with a childlike admiration. The truck eased itself into the rightmost lane, then up a ramp and into the back of a rest-area parking lot.

Drew got out without speaking, seemingly intent on what he was doing. But what, Cilla wondered, *was* he doing? First he checked all the mirrors. Then he leaned across the windshield and examined the wipers. Was there a problem? She hadn't noticed one, nor had Drew commented on anything being amiss.

Now he seemed to be checking the headlights.

When she got tired of wondering, she sat back more comfortably in her seat and switched on her e-book reader. As she read, she heard Drew open the gas-tank panel (they'd filled up thirty miles earlier—was he dusting for cobwebs or something?), and then she heard him undo the padlock on the back gate.

Ah, maybe that was it. Maybe he'd heard an "ominous thud"—like he had yesterday afternoon, when Cilla was at the wheel and he'd asked her to pull over. "I heard an ominous thud from the back," he'd explained, making her laugh with his choice of words. That particular thud had proved to be the result of a rubber tub full of kitchenware sliding off the tub below it and coming to rest decisively against a wooden bar stool.

She was startled into alertness by a politely restrained rapping on her window. Drew was looking up at her, with what her intimate knowledge of his face suggested was an odd combination of concern, troubleshooting efficiency...and mischief.

"Could you come around to the back for a minute?" He disappeared without waiting for an answer.

"What's up?" She stood beside him, peering into the open truck. If there was something wrong back here, she couldn't see what it was.

Drew just stared at her mysteriously. Again she noted the evidence, in his taut smile muscles, of a grin trying to fight its way forward.

"What?" she repeated. *"What?"*

He still didn't respond. The soupçon of smirkiness on his face remained.

"You do realize what time it is, don't you?" he finally said.

"Huh?" Cilla didn't see what difference the time made. She hadn't glanced at the dashboard clock since plunking her warm ass onto the chilly seat of the cab at 6:53 a.m. The clock was hard to see from the passenger seat, and the exact time was pretty meaningless to her, given that the day would be a nearly unbroken sequence of nearly identical hours of interstate-highway monotony. She knew it was morning; that was good enough for her.

But now she was intrigued. "Why? What time *is* it?"

His eyes flickered at her. "About five to eleven."

"Okay, so it's five to eleven. And...?"

"Five to *eleven*. Five to eleven on *Saturday*."

At last, the significance clicked. With all her fretting about absent routines today, how could she have forgotten to contemplate *this* one?

Elevenses: a term they'd picked up from the old British novels they loved—a quaint expression for a midmorning snack. Only for Cilla and Drew, the "snacking" had nothing to do with comestibles (except, as Drew had once pointed out while her head was in his lap, insofar as *comestibles* could be understood to include "come edibles"). *Elevenses*, in their weekend routine, was a sexual tide-me-over (or *bend-me-over* or sometimes *over and over*), for a couple whose appetites generally demanded satisfaction before noon rolled around.

Cilla sighed. "Ooh, yeah, elevenses," she said wistfully. "As if. Anyway, why are we standing here? Did you hear a noise?"

His blond bangs waved at her adorably when he shook his head. "Not yet. But I'm expecting to hear some nice sounds in a couple of minutes." He cocked his right eyebrow in the direction of the truck's interior.

The heat ignited in the little toe of her left foot—for some reason Cilla's most erogenous toe—and quickly rose to her crotch like water finding its level. "You're kidding," she said, hoping—and, in essence, knowing—that he wasn't.

"Why should I be kidding? It's time for elevenses, isn't it? And we have a private place behind a lockable door—and even the comfort of our very own bed."

She was already scrambling up onto the deck as he added, "As long as you can manage without your nightstand. I think that's buried under a carton or two of albums."

For the first time since they'd loaded up, Cilla looked into the transient, barely controlled chaos of the truck and saw it as home.

The bed—*their* bed—was boxed in among various other pieces of furniture. When they were loading it all in, she had told Drew that it looked like a "furniture party." But it was accessible, if one was motivated enough.

She was motivated.

"Wait a second!" Drew shouted with gleeful surprise when she climbed over their dresser and bounded down into the arena. "I was going to throw a spread over the mattress."

Cilla shrugged insouciantly.

"But you have the 'spread' thing covered, I guess."

It was true. Though she was still fully dressed in her jeans and tee, Cilla had spread-eagled herself on the bare mattress with all the enthusiasm of a woman reclaiming one of her favorite routines. She was a flexible girl, and her thighs were parted so wide, she could feel the seam of the denim threatening to rend.

Drew flicked on the overhead light and rattled the gate door shut. The reverberating *clang* it made when it hit the deck acted on Cilla like the shock of a wandering vibrator grazing an appreciative clit.

He took the trail she'd blazed—up and over the dresser—and landed neatly between her legs. She embraced him emphatically, warming her breasts against him, and his hard-on petitioned the fly of her jeans while he reached under to fondle the rounds of her asscheeks. When she raised her arms in invitation, he tickled her armpits with kisses, moistening the thin cotton of her T-shirt where it clung intimately to her sensitive hollows.

He flipped her over and she heard herself giggling, more than she had in days, as his cock sent further tickles of promise up and down her ass. Moments later, her jeans and panties were halfway down her thighs, and she sensed the undiluted focus of Drew's lust on her bare bottom. Though her face was to the mattress, she felt her consciousness mingling with her husband's in the crystal clarity of mutually understood desire.

He squeezed and slapped and nibbled, and she could feel her little bottom turning pink and warm and oh so fucking tingly-sweet. Her pussy was so slick now, her thighs slipped over each other like palms spreading suntan lotion.

Then Drew shuffled his own pants halfway down and lay naked-bellied on top of her, torso squishing her slap-sweetened buttocks, his skinny legs pressing on her nearly closed thighs... his cock just able to fit between them and tease the entrance to her cunt.

On one level, she wanted to stay in this position forever,

his rigid cylinder perfectly nestled against the give of her flesh, her pussy, ass and upper thighs a quivering territory of bare-skinned arousal that lay exposed between the hem of her tee and the crumpled jeans-and-panties border below. On one level, this was the ideal state of existence.

But, oh, she also wanted him inside her, wanted him to thrust inside her, wanted him to come inside her…wanted to let herself come with him inside her, and not before. So she wiggled an expressive wiggle that was slightly different from the way she'd been squirming in her heat, confident that Drew would know it meant the time had come to pull her pants off.

He shed his first. Cilla continued wiggling with anticipation while, over her shoulder, she watched him frantically dance and fumble himself free in the cramped space. Then she rolled onto her backside again, to finger her pussy and ogle the rugged frank-ness of Drew's ass as he bent to complete the task—balancing himself awkwardly against a floor lamp, whose presence added to the illusion that they were in their bedroom rather than the back of a truck.

When her own jeans and sneakers came off—Drew furrowing his brow with concentrated excitement as he tugged and twisted—Cilla reprised the spread-legged position she'd begun with, pried her fingers away from her dripping cunt…and waited to be fucked by her man, on her bed.

In a parking lot somewhere in Nebraska.

Neb-fucking-raska, maybe; but the word *home* fired through her horny brain as Drew smoothly entered her and drove his shaft *home*. He was completely at home in her cunt, and, god, he knew how to make her feel at home. Her muscles clamped hungrily around him, and she dragged her bottom up and down the contours of the naked mattress, letting jolts of sensation ping-pong from asscheeks to clit and back.

He filled her, unfilled her, refilled her...and it was so much pleasure she couldn't stand it, she was going to come—oh, yes, she was going to come wildly, and stain the mattress with sloppy pussy kisses.

Her clit grabbed the spark that was provided when Drew lingered, deliberately, on an upstroke, pressing the weight of his abdomen where he knew she'd thrill to it. He pinched her left nipple through soft cotton, and she heard herself moan out a lewd, throaty noise of deep release as a teetering wall of anticipation cracked into nuggets of ecstasy.

The heavy stem of the floor lamp made an ominous *thud* when she kicked it against the dresser in her throes. But Drew was coming hard, pinning her to the mattress as he filled her with hot comfort, and Cilla could not be bothered to concern herself with thuds, ominous or otherwise. Giving in to another aftershock of pleasure, her mind was on one thing only: this brand-new routine she'd call *road elevenses*—or, better yet, *elevenses on tour*. With a little careful planning, they could surely arrange to be at a rest area, service plaza, or truck stop at this same time tomorrow...and the next day...and the day after that...

NOON: LUNCHTIME RENDEZVOUS

Kat Watson

*D*ungeon, naked, 30 minutes.

Her text was simple, but I'd grown to expect her to behave just that way in moments like this. I knew from only those four words what she wanted. What she needed.

Squirming at my desk, I tried to focus on my work for the next twenty minutes. I was mostly unsuccessful, but I sent a few more emails, then let my assistant know I was leaving for lunch. One hour was all Alex had, but she'd make the most of it. We would make the most of it.

Almost the moment my knees hit the cold floor, my body naked and ready for her, the front door of our home opened and closed. Her shoes clicked against the wood, and I used the rhythm and sound to find the place I needed in my head. With my eyes lowered, I could only hear and smell her, sensing her movements around the room as she got ready.

Her toes appeared in front of me, and I smiled at the color on them from the pedicure we'd gotten together the previous weekend. She wrapped her fingers around my chin, lifting my head to look in my eyes.

"Ready, baby?"

Her eyes sparkled, almost daring me to say anything other than the affirmative. My smile broke across my face and I nodded, one quick tilt of my head.

"Up on the table."

I climbed up, facing the dark leather that covered the padded table. My wrists and ankles moved as she positioned them, locking them in place, opening my body for her pleasure. When she was done, her hands ran over my skin, warming and bringing it to life. I felt and heard the soft sound of fur against my ass and thighs. The sting increased when she switched toys, bringing a different sensation to my body and mind.

I climbed higher and deeper as she continued to play with me, to please herself, to release her mind from the binds it had no doubt been tangled in. My body responded to hers automatically, shifting into her movements, seeking the pleasure only she could bring me. Once my skin was hot, she ran the prickly tines of a metal wheel over the same areas, making me moan loudly. I wasn't embarrassed, not even for a minute—that was the exact purpose of this time between us. Pleasure. Sensation.

When she was satisfied with her progress, everything I had to offer reaffirmed as hers, she paused and unbound me.

"Turn over, my beautiful toy, it's my turn."

I gladly complied, eager to bring her the same levels of pleasure she so often brought me. My hands found their way around her body, pinching and pushing against her pliant flesh. When she lowered her pussy to my mouth, I eagerly lapped, sucked, and fucked. As she came quickly the first time, I felt a little smug. Her clit pulsed between my lips, a string of beautiful sounds flowing from her mouth.

"Again," she whispered.

Again, indeed. Again, and again, and again.

My fingers pushed into her carefully but steadily. I fucked her with my mouth, my fingers, my words. She rode my face for what felt like hours, but certainly was only a matter of minutes. I lost track of how many times she came, and then she turned above me. Her knees rested at my ears, her mouth poised exactly where I was desperate for her.

A single kiss to my clit was my only reward. I could have screamed in frustration.

"Thank you, pet. I'll meet you back here after work."

Her lithe body slid off mine, skin against skin, wasting no opportunity to tease and torture me more. I was so very fucked for working any more that day; my mind and body would not focus.

By the time I arrived back at our house, I was entirely on edge. I needed to come, I needed to release the day's stress, and pleasure her again. I ached for her.

Kneeling in my place, I listened when she arrived, and hoped. It was still entirely up to her if I had any release at all or if we'd simply focus on her needs again. Either way, I knew I'd be fine, but god, I hoped. I hoped with all I had.

"Bed," she said quietly, from somewhere else in the room.

Keeping my eyes lowered, I complied and lay on the soft bed. My eyes were closed, my breathing short and even in an attempt to keep calm. The anticipation of what she might do was nearly killing me. I could feel her as the end of the bed dipped, the fabric of the sheets touching and caressing her in ways I wanted to.

"Such a good girl," she cooed. "Thank you for pleasing me earlier. It's your turn now."

As her body moved above mine, my smile returned and

my eyes opened. I was grateful, but still curious what we were
going to do. Every way she pleased me was wonderful, but I still
wondered.

When she was face-to-face with me, her hands moved between
us, and the unmistakable cold of silicone pressed against me.
Her hips pushed forward, thrusting the fake cock as it nudged
between my pussy lips. Each time she pulled back and moved
forward, rubbing it right over and against my clit, I let out a soft
sound. She hadn't even fucked me yet and I was already so close
to the edge. Already whispering promises and begging.

"What a good slut you are," she whispered. "Wait for me."

Finally, she angled the cock and thrust inside me. Her pace
was relentless and hard, hitting exactly where I needed each
time. She fucked me for as long as she wanted, the minutes lost
to me as I held off my own orgasm, then her pace slowed. I could
tell she'd already come, the unmistakable sounds coming from
her as the other end of the device vibrated diligently against her
clit.

Mistress turned around again as she had earlier in the day
and plunged her tongue deep inside my pussy. She straddled my
face, and I pulled her down to me. Greedy and needing more of
her, I nipped at her thighs before I dove in. Somewhere between
fucking me and going down on me, she'd shed her harness.

I had a difficult time focusing with her demanding mouth
on my body, but I homed in on her, determined to make her
come again before I did. There was no way I could fail this task.
My fingers toyed with her swollen lips, then two of my fingers
dipped into her. I fucked her hard, at precisely the angle and
depth I knew from years of experience drove her wild. I almost
didn't hear her when she breathed out a short "Now."

Her fingers and mouth worked together as she came, and I
envied her. I had no idea how she could focus on both tasks,

my arms and body tightening as I came, rendering me inca-
pable of paying proper attention to her. My mouth continued
to lavish her with affection as we both came down. I kissed her
thighs, her clit, everywhere I could reach. When she was sated,
she pulled up and away from me.

The sound of the shower in the next room pulled me from
my haze of floating, and I joined her there. It was usually a
transitional room for us, a space to get clean, talk about what
we'd done, and remember what we were to each other the other
75 percent of our relationship. She was my wife, my love, my
everything.

ONE P.M.
TEST DRIVE

Angell Brooks

There. He just did it again." Carly strained her neck to watch Eli walk away. "Mmm, that man does have a nice ass on him."

"He did what exactly, Carly?" Trish's voice sounded weary. It had been a hellish day so far, and all she wanted to do was get through the next four hours without killing someone. After that, it was a long bus ride home to a hot bath, yoga pants and an *NCIS* marathon on her PVR. And wine. Lots of wine.

She sighed to herself as she straightened out the leasing papers in front of her. She felt like she was sixty instead of thirty-two. But with no social life to speak of, she was beginning to consider getting a cat, or two, and accepting her fate as an old maid.

"Earth to Trish. Where did you disappear to?" Carly's face popped into her field of vision. Trish shook her head. "Sorry. Just drifted. What did you say?"

"I *said* he undressed you with his eyes, again." That gave Trish a good chuckle. "Oh, Carly. Seriously? He's what, twenty-four? And hot. *And* let's not forget, the youngest GM in the history of Liberty Lexus. Besides, we've been friends for years. That's as far as it goes."

Her heart sank a little at the truth to those words. But she was ancient in comparison to half the females on staff. *And they're all a hundred times more beautiful*, she thought as Mary-Anne from accounting walked by, waving a perfectly manicured hand cheerfully. Carly snorted, watching Mary-Anne stop in front of Eli's door, smoothing out her pencil skirt and giving her perfectly round (and fake) 38Ds an un-needed adjustment.

Trish's hands went to her own wrinkled polyester nightmare flare skirt—the only thing clean in the closet this morning—and silently bemoaned her lack of discipline in getting to the gym.

Carly watched her friend with a combination of sadness and amusement. Trish thought she was over-the-hill, and often dressed the part. But with her large, coffee-colored eyes, tawny hair and plump lips, she was, in Carly's opinion, a million times more beautiful and sexy than the Barbie dolls that Eli had been hiring lately.

Although word through the company grapevine was that none of them had managed to even get close to a date with the charismatic GM. Which left the field wide open for Trish to give it her best shot, if she ever decided to try. Because despite her denial, Carly could read the signs. And she'd be willing to bet a month's salary that Eli had a hard-on for her friend as well.

Unaware of the personal assessment being given in Carly's mind, Trish double-checked her schedule in front of her and cursed under her breath. "Shit. I completely forgot about that." She marched over to Eli's door, pausing briefly when she heard the annoying giggle coming from behind it. "Eli." She announced herself loudly before walking in. "Mr. Alvers is going to be here at two o'clock to see the new RX450 and no one has taken it on a test drive yet." She glared pointedly at Mary-Anne, who had balanced a slender hip on the corner of Eli's desk and was leaning in flirtatiously. "I know you're the boss, but it still needs to be taken care of. And since Mr. Alvers is not only one of our richest clients, but also one of our best…"

"I'll take care of it myself, Trish." Eli's voice was neither strained nor harried. In fact, it seemed a little grateful. He pushed away from his desk. "Mary-Anne, we'll go over those numbers tomorrow morning." He turned, obviously dismissing her. Sighing, she pouted and flounced away, like a petulant child who was told she couldn't play with her favorite toy.

Trish followed, smiling to herself. If she didn't know any better, she'd think that the boss was trying to get away from the overzealous junior accountant. She grabbed the keys off her desk and handed them to him. "Enjoy. It's a gorgeous day for a ride."

"So come with me."

Trish's eyes widened in shock. "But I, um…"

Carly nudged her. "She'd love to. She needs to get out of here." And before Trish could protest again, she was out the front door and climbing into the passenger seat of the luxury SUV.

She sat back, inhaling the new-car smell. The leather seats cradled her aching back and ass, and she moaned quietly. "Oh yeah, that's the stuff."

Eli watched as she settled, sinking into the plush interior like she owned it. His cock stirred in his pants as his gaze traveled down to her curvy legs, crossed at the ankles in cheap shoes and hose. Trish had put in her time with the company, but was always getting overlooked for the glamour girls—they were what management called "good P.R."

But Trish, well, she was quality and proof that women do get better with age. They'd become friends six years ago, when he'd started washing cars in the dealership's bays. She was hot then, but he'd been looking to his future. He'd kept his head down and learned all he could about the business. He was driven and ambitious and nothing was going to get in his way. When he received his promotion four months ago, he knew he'd earned it. And somehow, he was going to use his position to help her out.

"Eli?" He looked up into Trish's amused gaze. "Are we going for that test drive or not?" Suddenly feeling like he was eighteen again, he fumbled with the key ring. She laughed as he remembered about the keyless start and hit the button. As he took a deep breath to calm himself, he managed to slide the key fob easily into the ignition. He flashed to an image of sliding into Trish that easily and his cock throbbed.

Instead of concentrating on that, he turned on the stereo and pulled the car out of the lot and into traffic. Trish started tapping her nails in time to the beat, and she had put her window down to enjoy the fresh summer air. He smiled to himself, and enjoyed the open road. He drove around the block a few times, testing the brakes, listening to the transmission shift, and letting the car talk to him.

Driving along the deserted side streets behind the dealership, he passed an empty field. The tapping had stopped a while ago and was replaced with the sounds of small, even breaths. He smiled. Trish had taken advantage of the reclining seats and was fast asleep.

Pulling into one of the parking lots, he stopped the car suddenly, causing her to lurch forward. "What the fuc...Eli!" He parked the car, turning to her. As she rubbed the back of her neck, glaring at him, he removed his seat belt and un-clicked hers too.

"Come on. Get out." He left his door open, walking around

to her side of the car. "You're driving." Ushering her out of her seat, he slid in, leaving her no other option but to take the wheel.

"Why are you doing this?" As she adjusted the seat, her voice shook. This was a luxury vehicle, about forty thousand dollars above her pay grade. What if she fucked it up?

"Because, Trish, you are going to be presenting this car to Mr. Alvers, and I expect you to be able to talk from experience. First thing you need to know is how she handles."

Her eyes wide, Trish just sat in shock. "Why am *I* presenting the car to Mr. Alvers?" She faced front, her hands on her face. "I can't do it. I just can't. Eli, I don't know the first thing about presenting...anything."

"Trish. You've driven cars before. This is exactly the same as any other. They all have the same parts. So just drive." As she pulled out of the parking spot and onto the road, he continued, "You've worked your ass off at the store. You've held it together through two presidents and three GMs. You know that place inside and out. You deserve a promotion, and this little baby here is going to help you get it. When you present it to Mr. Alvers, he's going to be impressed by you. And then he'll mention it to Jonathan over golf, who will then ask me about you, and I can give you a *glowing* recommendation."

She grinned at the thought.

"Turn here." Eli indicated the empty field. "We'll take her off-roading and see what she can really do." Trish followed his instructions, keeping it steady over the bumps and divots in the dirt. He indicated a ramshackle shed. "Pull over there."

When she had it in park, she sat back and laughed. "You know, Eli, that was the most fun I've had in a long time. Thanks." She grinned over at him, the laugh dying in her throat. His gaze was intense, like he wanted to have her for breakfast. "Eli?" She fidgeted with her seat belt, suddenly very aware of where she was. In an empty field. In an SUV. With the hottest guy she'd ever known.

Alone.

Instead of answering, he got out of the car. She did the same, walking around the back to meet him halfway. His hands reached for her, one snaking around the back of her neck, the other to her back. In one swift move he had her pressed against him. "I've wanted to do this for a very, very long time." His lips fell on hers, gently at first, testing the waters. She stood frigid, not sure of what to do. Inside, Eli panicked. *What if she slaps me? Did I just fuck up?*

And then, with a sigh, Trish let herself go. Her arms wound around him and she pulled him closer. Her tongue played against his lips with a fervor that shocked him and surprised her. But he caught on quick enough, tangling his hand in her hair with years of pent-up passion and frustration.

Her hands fell lower on his body, exploring that fine ass that Carly had been lusting over earlier in the day. Tight and muscular, she noted, as his lips left hers to trail her neck. He reached beneath her blouse to fondle her breasts through her black lace bra.

Her nails raked down his shirt, feeling the muscles coil tightly beneath her fingertips. He gasped, his hard-on pressing against her thigh. From what she could feel, his cock was long, not too long, but thick. She groaned at the thought of it inside her and rubbed against it, making him gasp again. This was one of her wildest dreams, and even then she never believed it could happen.

Eli pulled away from her. Clearing his throat, he backed away slowly, snapping his cuffs. *Shit*, Trish thought. *He's sorry he did it.* Not wanting to be the first one to speak, she made a big show of straightening her stockings.

"So, Trish. Now that you've opened her up on the road, let's open her up in back." He pushed the button to release the hatch. "After all, you can tell Mr. Alvers that she handles like a dream on pavement. Shouldn't you also know about the car's interior?" As the hatch rose to its full height, she noticed that the back seats had been put down. Taking her hand in his, Eli raised it to his lips, placing a kiss in the very center of it. "Example, there's plenty of room in the cargo space."

She trembled when she realized what he was asking. "It looks so roomy. I wonder if I could lie down back there and take a nap—you know, like on a day trip or if I went camping?" He guided her forward to the opening. "Let's find out, shall we?"

She crawled in, lying down as Eli followed and closed the hatch. He hovered next to her, a devilish smile crossing his features. Leaning down, he kissed her again, his tongue plunging into her mouth, skipping off hers. His hands traveled under her skirt, his fingers stroking her heated pussy through her thin panties. She reached for his crotch and returned the favor, outlining his hard length with her nails.

She gazed around. "Well, there seems to be a lot of space from this angle. But I'm short. I'm wondering, if I had something taller than me, would it fit comfortably?" she questioned coyly. Grabbing his shirt front, she pulled him in for a quick, liquid kiss. "In case you didn't get it, *Mr.* Greyson," she whispered. "I'm wondering how comfortable a man would be if he was between my legs, with his face buried in my..." Her voice caught on the last word.

Eli grinned and chuckled as he eased himself on top of her. "I believe, Trish, that the word you're looking for is *pussy*." His touch was light, sliding the silken material down her thighs and off, tossing them into the window well. His head disappeared under her skirt. "And I guess we'll just have to find out."

She tensed in anticipation. His fingers gently parted her lips, the tip of his tongue tracing a line from her hole to her hood, flicking at her swollen clit. Shuddering, Trish mewed. He drew patterns in the thin layer of moisture, feeling it thicken with her excitement. His cock felt uncomfortably huge pressed against the floor and he shifted to take the pressure off. But the motion caused his briefs to rub against the shaft in a very pleasurable way and he bit back a groan.

She reached down, running her fingers through his once perfectly coiffed hair before grabbing it in fistfuls and guiding his mouth back to her. "Please tell me that's not all you've got." With his face forced against her mound, his nose brushed against her when he shook his head. Her giggle turned to a gasp when his teeth nipped at her labia. Slowly, as not to distract her, he slid two fingers into her waiting heat. Curving them, he rocked against her front wall, feeling her control beginning to break as her muscles gripped the invading digits.

He moved to her clit, his tongue following a rhythm all its own. *Flick, flick, lick, lick, graze, breathe and repeat.* Trish's head rocked side to side, tears leaking down her cheeks, as she lost her breath to the pleasure. Her whole body practically vibrated as he kept her on the edge of what she was sure would be the biggest orgasm she was ever going to have.

"Please, Eli." She practically sobbed. "Please, make me come."

His mouth stretched in a self-satisfied grin, he replied, "Well, since you said *please*." His fingers began thrusting and he fastened his lips to her bud, sucking in quick bursts. His tongue was assaulted by her sweet rush of release as she came with a warrior's cry.

With her disembodied voice ringing through the car, her

whole world exploded. Where once she had a skeleton, she now had Jell-O. Her body trembled and shook, falling apart at the seams so completely she was worried that she'd never be able to put herself back together again. As she came down, breathing in gasps, Eli gently pulled away, moving up to lie down next to her.

Leaning over her on one elbow, his free hand caressed her hard nipples through her blouse. She turned to look at him, a vixen's smile playing over her swollen lips. "So, did you have enough room down there?" For a second he thought she was making a comment about her still-twitching pussy and was about to defend it, but then he realized she meant in terms of the cargo space itself.

"Oh yes. Plenty of room. It was very," he leaned in to kiss her, "very comfortable. Were you, um, comfortable?"

She purred, reaching over, her hand resting on his cock. "Yes, yes I was." Intent on unzipping his pants, she saw his watch. "Um, Eli? What time is the appointment with Mr. Alvers?"

"Two o'clock. There's plenty of..." She turned his wrist so he could see the time. "*Shit!*"

In a tangle of arms and legs they managed to find their way out of the cargo space and into the front seats. Eli jammed the car into drive and pulled a 180 that would have made most stunt drivers jealous.

Straightening out her blouse and smoothing down her skirt, Trish was sure her face would give her away when she walked in. "Eli..." she began.

"Trish." He interrupted her. "I know how your mind works, and before you say another word, know this." He glanced over at her. "I did this because I wanted to—because I want you. So don't overthink it."

He pulled into the parking lot in a squeal of tires and brakes.

Rushing around to her side, he helped her out of the car, pressing something into her hands as he did. She knew the scrap of material was her thong, and she pushed it into her purse.

"Now keep cool."

As they walked into the service entrance, Carly called over. "Oh guys, Mr. Alvers canceled. He rescheduled for tomorrow, and he no longer wants the RX450. Now he's interested in the LX570. That means another test drive."

Trish and Eli looked at each other and grinned. As she brushed past him to get to her desk she murmured in his ear, "Tomorrow it's your turn."

TWO P.M.
BIKER BAR

Thomas S. Roche

Summer and I have a little game we like to play in the afternoon—always in the afternoon, because that's when she gets horny. Summer always gets *impossibly* horny in the afternoon.

When she started her two o'clock promises, we'd been together about three months. She'd started a new job as a physical therapist, in which she almost always worked Sundays; double-time was hard to turn down. We only got one complete day a week together, Saturday. We're both very social people, and we like to socialize together. Not hanging out with our friends together was, and is, as unthinkable as not making love.

Trying to get a week's worth of socializing and foreplay, all on a Saturday, can be hard.

So lately, we combine the two.

The first time she gave me a two o'clock promise, it started not on Saturday afternoon but Thursday night—about ten or eleven. That's when she laid the groundwork. I'd given her a spanking that left her round, tight bottom rather red. We were fooling around, and she asked me if I'd ever done anal. *Yes.* She asked me if I'd liked it. *YES.* She asked me if I wanted to do it again. *YES, YES, YES.*

"Why?" I asked her. "Are you interested?"

She made a face.

"No," she said, somewhat harshly. "It must hurt."

"Not if you do it right," I said.

"Well, I'm not into that. It's perverted."

She sounded borderline pissed, which surprised me.

"Okay," I said. "No problem. You know we don't ever have to do anything you're not into."

It was Thursday night, and she'd let me spank her, and there was a nice warm perfect pair of buns for my hands to caress. I did this, and she and I went back to making slow, soft, tired, late-evening Thursday night love. She got pretty into it.

I would even go so far as to say that Summer seemed more turned on than usual. Which is saying a lot; saying Summer's an enthusiastic lover is the understatement of the century.

Fast-forward to Saturday afternoon. We have this group of friends who always meets at Schadenfreude on Valencia Street. I'll tell you it's a biker bar, but don't get the wrong idea; these aren't exactly Hells Angels. You'll see more BMWs and Ducatis parked outside than you will Harley-Davidsons. Schadenfreude has heat lamps and Burning Man surplus umbrellas and something like fifty beers on tap. It's got a huge backyard that's sweet as hell to hang in when the weather's nice. That Saturday, the weather was nice.

I don't remember who all was there that day—Joey and Courtney, for sure, and Amy and Keith K and Jeff Morales probably, and Rich and Stan might have been there; sometimes they bring friends along. I think that might have been the day Gabriel Pacheco and his crew rode up from Sunnyvale, like they do sometimes. They'll do it when it's raining, even; those Sunnyvale cats are crazy. Like I said, Schadenfreude has heat lamps and umbrellas over the picnic tables on the patio, so apparently it's the number-one choice of people who would drip on the floor if given half a chance. How those freaks keep their cigarettes dry, I'll never know.

Anyway, so I don't remember exactly who was there, but I remember everything else that matters. I remember Summer had on her low-cut T-shirt in this burgundy color that set off her eyes and a V-neck that set off her tits—I'm equally fond of both pairs of fetching attributes. She wore faded blue jeans with a little flare to the leg—a few years out of fashion, but who gives a shit? I remember the flare of the legs and the tight-ish cut across her ass; *hot*. Her buns looked eminently spankable, as they usually do. She had on sort of wedge heels, which gave those flare legs even more of a seventies look. Her long blond hair was rumpled and unkempt; it had the freshly fucked look. We'd had a nice long slow morning waking up together, but she refused to get me off. "Save it," she told me. And she wouldn't come, either. We'd spent a couple hours making out and fooling around, and then she leapt off me and threw her clothes on without showering, demanding brunch.

So I was already more than a little horny. Little did I know this was all in Summer's plan. She'd had been planning her devious scene since Thursday, so this morning wasn't even the start of making me "save it."

Like I said, I don't remember exactly who was there, but we were seated at the splintery picnic table, and it was a big crowd, and the weather was gorgeous. I do remember the beer was a dollar off in honor of this guy who'd gotten killed on the MacArthur Freeway.

Someone passed around a joint. That's basically okay there as long as you know whoever's tending bar and keep an eye out not for the cops but for the Environmental Sensitivity complainants, who will lecture your ass till Sunday morning about toxins and free radicals. Don't get me wrong, I'm highly sympathetic to their plight. After all, my significant other has another kind of environmental sensitivity; afternoon sunlight makes her horny.

Anyway, Summer took a hit—just one, I watched her—and I passed, since I was driving. Mind you, I'm not pulling my Responsible Citizen card out of my pants; there were already two beers and a shot of Bulleit inside me. In addition to the pot, there was an indeterminate number of pinot blancs inside Summer; Schadenfreude is the rare bar in the States where you can get the latter by the glass. Funny thing about bikers nowadays; they no longer know where to get the cheapest methamphetamine, but if the white you want comes in a glass, look for the guys in Vanson leathers cracking jokes about Google Plus.

Anyway, we'd been there for an hour, and our original plan was to stay for two. I already knew Summer gets extremely horny in the afternoon, starting about two o'clock. And when Summer's horny, I'm horny. But I didn't yet know that she planned to play a game with me.

About two o'clock, she leaned over and whispered in my ear: "Baby, I'm horny."

I smiled and patted her leg. I kissed her, trying to be reasonably discreet.

"Wanna go home and fuck?" she whispered.

I leaned in and said, "Let's finish our drinks."

What reason was there to rush? We'd head home about three and have the rest of the afternoon to—

Summer leaned in closer and purred in my ear with a low, soft heat.

"I'll *do things* for you," she told me.

I gave her a look.

"What kind of things," I said out loud.

"Dirty things," she whispered.

This time *I* whispered, too. "What kind of dirty things?" I asked her, smelling her hair—shampoo and sex.

She gave me the innocent, wide-eyed gaze of the coquette, tossing her freshly fucked hair. She looked shy and dirty at the same time—and most of all, she looked seductive.

"I don't know," she said, no longer whispering but speaking in a low enough voice that no one else noticed. "I can't imagine what filthy, perverted things men like you might want to do to girls."

I looked at her incredulously. Her hand traced a path up my blue-jeaned thigh, just far enough under the table that no one could see. My cock began stiffening.

Mind you, if she'd said she wanted to go home because she had a headache or otherwise wasn't feeling well, I would have loaded her on my bike and gotten her home and put her to bed. But I could see that sparkle in her bright green eyes, and I knew I wanted to make them sparkle more. More than just a simple response like taking her home and fucking her would have.

So I smiled and told her, "Just let me finish my beer."

She gave me a petulant look that had a couple of friends around the table asking what was wrong. Summer has big, full lips, and when she sticks that bottom one out she looks very much like a pouting schoolgirl who needs to be spanked, which wasn't that far off the mark. "Nothing's wrong," I told them good-naturedly. "Except my girlfriend's a brat sometimes."

They all agreed, and asserted that they all liked her that way and I liked her that way most of all, while Summer nonetheless pouted still more and said her reputation was being impugned and she wouldn't stand for it. But her response was to stamp her foot, which only made her seem more petulant and bratty, which I liked.

Everything died down for a minute while we chatted and sipped our drinks. Summer's hand remained on my thigh, keeping me roughly at half-mast with an almost imperceptible motion of her fingertips without *quite* crossing the line of propriety.

Then, when everything was more or less back to baseline calm (for Schadenfreude, at least), she leaned in close and whisper-growl-whimpered in my ear again.

"You can take me over your lap," she said.

I looked at her, flat and unaffected—but she could feel my body shifting at the rise of my cock in my jeans.

She put her lips back at my ear and breathed warmly: "And spank me."

She pulled back and looked at me, eyes big and bright, mouth round in an innocently naïve expression.

"If you wanna," she mewled.

I wasn't all the way hard then, but Summer was. Her arousal was palpable and, more to the point, visible. To use a trashy metaphor, she had her high beams on—and it wasn't because of the breeze coming off the bay. Remember that burgundy top I described? Her nipples distended its front quite adorably.

At that point I would have just about put her in a headlock to get her home, if that's what it took. But I sensed that she was playing a game, and I smiled and said, "As soon as I finish my beer."

She pouted some more, and slipped one foot out of its wedge heel, and leaned over and ran it up and down my calf. It wasn't where no one could see, but nobody at our table could. People at other tables could have seen what she was up to, if they'd bothered to look.

There passed another few minutes of casual conversation, while I sensed the building energy in Summer's body. It wasn't just that she wanted to fuck; it was that she wanted to say something.

She even started it several times, leaning over and breathing hot and humid in my ear, then pulling back and blushing and saying, "Nevermind." If I hadn't been familiar with that playful look in Summer's eyes, I would have just taken her home.

But I wanted to know what was on her mind.

We played the game for another ten minutes, pretending like everything was normal. Then Summer finally leaned in and gave it to me: the card she'd had up her sleeve since Thursday night.

It came out hot and wet, with the graze of her lips and even her tongue, a little, up against my earlobe. Her breath made the back of my neck goose-bump. Her voice was a sexual organ in itself, especially with what she told me.

"You could put it in my butt," she said.

I looked at her, incredulous.

Again, the coquette look: innocent, flirtatious, naïve.

She leaned in close again.

"If you wanna," she said. "I know bad men like you wanna do that to girls. Gross things like that. I'm just so *horny*... I think I'd let you do *anything*..."

She was already winning the game, and we both knew it. I was fully hard now. Her hand rested silent in the shadows under the table, her fingertips just grazing my swelling jeans.

I went to take a sip of beer.

Summer's lips made it to my ear before the glass made it to my lips.

She whispered, "If you take me home *right now*, you can *spank me*...and fuck me...and *fuck my ass*... You perverted weirdo, I know you wanna do that stuff, and if I wasn't so horny, I wouldn't—I'd never—but I've just *got* to get fucked, I'm so horny, mister, I—"

I shivered all over and slammed the last third of my beer.

I grabbed for my jacket and held it in front of me as I stood.

"I think Summer and I are gonna head home," I said. "Didn't get much sleep last night…"

"I *bet* you didn't!" someone said, and there was laughter. Summer looked like the cat that ate the canary.

Summer sauntered with painful slowness, taking her time giving hugs all around the table while I stood in hard-on distress near the exit.

Once she nabbed the canary, a girl like Summer can't resist playing with her food.

She let me do it—spank her and fuck her and fuck her in the ass. She made good on her promise, telling me the whole time about how she'd never do something like this, but she was just so horny. Her disgust was all an act. She'd done it before. She liked it. In fact, she still asks for it regularly—but only when she's so horny she has to get fucked right away. Those times, she knows she has to promise me something "really dirty" to get me to give her what she needs—and fast.

But that was just the first of Summer's two o'clock promises, and there've been many since. It turns out there's a lot of things she's done that she didn't tell me about. She let me do them to her for the first time all over again. There are other things she's never done, that she wants to do, but pretends she doesn't. She lets me do those to her, too.

But only when she's so afternoon-horny that she simply *has* to get fucked, and fast.

Some of those are really, really dirty.

Way dirtier than what we did that first time.

Way dirtier.

Whenever Summer puts her lips to my ear in the afternoon, I know I'm going to get a promise. Whenever she breathes out secrets and promises in that breathy, horny voice, I know I'm about to get a two o'clock promise.

And it's always something *good*.

THREE P.M.
CLOSED-DOOR
MEETING

Sasha White

Some say absence makes the heart grow fonder. I say absti-
nence makes the lust burn hotter. This is the reason I don't
begrudge the fact that my husband occasionally travels for his
work. Michael, my brainy geophysicist, whose studious glasses
and button-up shirts hide the fiery libido of a hot-blooded syba-
rite, never fails to feed my hunger for him while he is away, or
satisfy it completely upon his return.

And with his return from Cairo only two days away, I ignored
everyone and everything outside my office doors and strove to
get all my accounts caught up so I could be free to welcome
him home for a long weekend. Only instead of the columns
and numbers on the pages in front of me, my mind was full
of images of greeting him at the airport, being swept up in his
strong arms and held against his muscled body. The drive home
would be silent, ripe with anticipation that hardened my nipples
and moistened my thighs. Barely inside the doors of our home
he would shove me against the wall, rough in his eagerness—

eagerness that flowed hotly through my own blood as he'd lift my skirts, make quick work of his zipper before thrusting home. A quick hard fuck, animalistic in its intent and action.

Yes, my geeky husband would let loose his true desires, mastering me completely as he'd take me again and again, keeping me naked and wet as he used my body and reconnected our souls.

As if conjured by my lustful thoughts, my husband's handsome face came up on my twenty-inch screen, and a telltale pinging brought me up short. With barely a glance at the clock I accepted the call. "What's wrong?" I asked before Michael could say anything. It was just after three in the afternoon for me, which meant after midnight for him. An unusual time for him to make contact.

"Just missing you," he said, his voice husky, his smile sleepy.

I drank in the sight of stubbled jaw and heavy-lidded eyes, only then realizing that my heart had been in my throat. "Lord, Michael, you scared me, calling so late." He was a scientist visiting a university, not a soldier searching through dangerous tunnels for terrorists, but I still worried when he wasn't by my side.

He ran a hand through his adorably rumpled hair and frowned apologetically. "Sorry, I was dreaming and woke up wanting you. I'll let you get back to work."

"Don't you dare hang up, mister!" I said quickly. "I was just surprised because of the time. You know I'm always eager to see you."

"Forty-nine more hours until you'll be seeing me in person," he said. The camera shifted and then settled, filling my screen with the delicious sight of my husband's completely naked form, sprawled amidst rumpled bedsheets. The heat that had pooled low in my belly during my earlier thoughts reignited, spreading fast when his cock waved at me.

"You are missing me, aren't you, darling?"

"I am." He stroked himself lightly, making my mouth water. "It's been three weeks since this has been buried deep in your juicy cunt. Remind me why I took this gig?"

His crude words had my sex clenching hungrily, and I fought to speak coherently. "Money, prestige, a need to share your beautiful mind with the rest of the world."

He shook his head, laughter shining in his slumberous eyes. "Oh, yeah. What was I thinking?"

"You were probably thinking that it would be okay because when you got home your wife would be eager to make up for lost time on her knees, and we both know how much you enjoy that."

His laugh was husky. "Just as we both know how much you do."

"Only two more days, Michael, then that'll be my hand stroking your flesh." I stared into the tiny camera at the top of my computer screen and licked my lips. "Or my mouth."

He groaned. "I was hoping to catch you alone. Why don't you slide your chair back and lift your skirt for me?"

My nipples hardened and my breath caught. "Let me lock the door," I said, pushing my chair back to stand.

"No. Leave it."

I froze at his command. "Michael, I can't—"

"Yes, you can. It's closed, right? Mornings you keep it open, afternoons you keep it closed so you can get shit done."

A shiver of excitement danced down my spine as I stared at my closed office door. Normal, everyday business sounds could be heard through the door, muffled, but still there. I was no angel, as Michael well knew, and while a little risk always made hot sex go supernova, this was my office. If someone walked in, it would be someone I knew, not some random stranger.

"C'mon, Katherine," Michael's voice whispered out of the computer. "Show me the naughty girl that's buried beneath that straitlaced business suit."

Tearing my gaze from the door, I stood and angled the computer screen so it was directly in front of me and tilted slightly down. After shrugging off the jacket of my suit I skimmed my hands over my aching breasts, cupping them, thumbs rubbing over the nipples briefly before traveling down over my hips to slowly slide the pencil skirt I was wearing upward. On screen Michael watched, eyes glued to my hands as I raised my skirt inch by inch, his own hand gripping his rigid cock.

"There's my girl," he crooned when he saw the top of my stockings and the garter belt that held them up. I spread my thighs and lifted the skirt that final inch that showed him the bare flesh of my thighs and the fine hairs covering my pussy. "I love that you never wear panties. You're always ready to go, aren't you?"

"Only for you."

"Touch yourself," he said. "Are you wet for me now?"

Shifting my stance, I dipped a hand between my thighs and ran a finger over the swollen lips of my cunt, teasing myself as Michael liked to tease me. A quick foray with two fingers proved I was indeed ready, and I lifted my hand to the screen, showing him the gleaming juices coating them.

"Taste yourself. Lick your fingers clean, and imagine it's my mouth on them. My tongue swirling over them and reveling in your flavor."

A whimper of pleasure rose in my throat and my knees weakened at the desire shining in Michael's eyes. Once again, as if reading my mind, my husband told me to sit. "Show me how you miss me, my love."

Needing no further encouragement, I sank back into my

chair and began to play. As I made quick work of the buttons on my silk blouse, a brief prayer of thanks for the advances in modern technology drifted through my mind. Not only could I view my husband's prime form even while thousands of miles away, but in a smaller window, on the bottom of the computer screen, I could see my own.

The sides of my blouse were pushed aside and I could almost feel the heat of his gaze on my generous breasts. On the screen the deep red of my ripe nipples was visible through the lace of my bra. With a flick of my hand the front clasp was undone and I shoved the cups away, exposing myself.

"Pinch your nipples," my husband commanded. "Imagine your fingers are my teeth."

I did as he asked, watching as he licked his lips, the hand stroking his cock tightening. "Cup your balls," I ask. "Imagine it's my hand between your thighs."

Michael spreads his legs and his second hand delves between them. The palm of my hand itches to touch him. Instead, I spread my thighs further and lift my feet to place them on the edge of the desk.

"Can you see me?" I ask, even though the small image on my screen assures me my chair is far enough from the desk that he can. I lower my hand and brush my fingertips over the sparse curls on my mound. "Do you see the shine of my juices on my lips? See how wet just the sight of you, the sound of your voice, makes me?"

The shrill ring of a phone shattered our solitude at the exact moment I ran a finger up and down my slit and I jolted, causing my finger to delve deeper even as I tensed in fear.

Neither of us moved as the line was picked up outside my door. When the phone on my desk didn't ring again I knew the call wasn't for me, and relief softened my muscles.

Michael's chuckle brought a flush of embarrassed excitement to my cheeks and a wash of cream to my cunt. I smiled at him. "You're going to get me fired," I whispered as I fingered myself.

"If anyone walked in on you they'd only drool at the sight of your lusciousness."

Saliva filled my mouth. "Like I'm drooling at the sight of yours?" I asked.

He changed angles so I could better see his engorged cock, his fist moving steadily over it. "I can't wait to feel your drool greasing my dick as I fuck your mouth. That's what I was dreaming of that woke me."

"It's what I was thinking of just before you called," I said, rubbing a fingertip over my clit. Little shocks of pleasure whipped from clit to nipples and back to the curl into the tight knot of desire deep within my belly. "I dreamed of greeting you at the airport, of feeling your arms around me. The exquisite tension building between us as you drove us home, only to break when we entered the house and you shoved me against the wall and buried your cock deep inside me."

His groan rumbled from the speakers, filling the small office and causing my eyes to jump to the door and my pulse to jump. The shadow of feet passed under the door and my insides clenched around my finger. Adding another I thrust deep and fast, matching pace with my husband's strokes.

"After fucking you hard against the wall, you'd get on your knees." He took up my fantasy and continued in a rough voice. "Your lips would lick your own juices from my cock, cleaning me, then taking me deep into your mouth and sucking until I was hard again. I'd wrap my fingers in your hair and watch as your cheeks hollowed and filled with every thrust."

I forgot about teasing him with words as his own aroused me

beyond control. Lust swamped me and I fucked myself harder, frigging my clit with the fingers of my other hand as my gaze stayed glued to the screen filled with my husband's burning eyes and swollen cock. The head angry and red, the veins visible as he pumped his fist fast and hard, bringing his own sexual juices to the tip.

Hunger for his taste filled my soul and I whimpered. God, I missed him. I wanted him, I craved his touch, his taste...his body inside mine as we connected in the most basic way. The slickness of my need flooded my thighs as our eyes met; it was as if there were nothing between us, and when his lips parted and his command reached my ears, my body obeyed. "Come for me, wife."

Heart pounding in my chest, I bit my lip to muffle my cries as the burning ball of lust in my belly exploded and pleasure singed every nerve in my body. My thighs trembled and my senses filled with the vision of my husband's cock jerking. I was so into it that I could smell him, taste him, even as his grunts of release echoed in my head.

Much sooner than I would've liked, the real world intruded in the form of loud voices just outside my door. I quickly dropped my feet to the floor, did up my bra and blouse while Michael's satisfied laughter caressed my ears. "You are such a naughty, naughty woman, Katherine. So prim and proper, and yet so delicious in your desires."

My own satisfaction weighed down my limbs as I smiled at him. "And you so clever and canny in your own work, yet so down and dirty in heart."

Our eyes met as the phone on my desk began to ring. "We are a pair, aren't we?" he asked.

"We are the best pair," I replied as someone else picked up the office line again.

"I know you have to go back to work," he said. "Thank you for indulging me this afternoon."

The phone beeped and a tinny voice filled the room. "Line two is for you, Katherine."

I looked at the clock on the computer screen, then back at my husband. "Forty-eight hours and twenty minutes until I see you again."

"Then we'll do this for real."

The phone beeped the angry tone of a call on hold for too long, and my finger hovered over the handset. "Love you," I said.

He smiled and set his head on his pillow. "Love you, too."

The screen went blank and I steeled myself. Picking up the phone, determination mixed with love.

Forty-eight hours and nineteen minutes left.

FOUR P.M.
NO-SHOW

Cora Zane

R ain drenched the afternoon in a solid sheet of gray. From Elise's perch behind the front counter of the occult shop, she listened to the rumbling thunder and stared through the display window, watching the downpour. The dreary weather showed no signs of letting up. Slow moving and determined, the traffic stuttered along Decatur Street, a cautious chain of headlights and brake lights blending into a steady stream. She sighed. *No one is going out in that mess unless they have to.*

Restless and a little disappointed, she tapped her yellow highlighter against the appointment book on the counter. She hated to mark off another no-show, but she checked the wall clock again and saw it was already after four p.m. Her last scheduled client for the afternoon should have arrived thirty minutes ago.

She didn't usually get a lot of people in for tarot sessions on Mondays, but one of her regular clients had booked a reading weeks in advance. The woman never showed up late, but at the same time, she hadn't called in, so Elise didn't know what to think. She had prepared for a busy afternoon, and earlier spent a good twenty minutes setting up the private consultation room in the back, lighting candles and incense, and pulling the silky, patchwork drapes closed in an effort to create an atmosphere some of her clients seemed to expect when paying by the hour to have their cards read. However, it looked like she wouldn't need the room after all.

"To heck with it..." She marked the no-show off the list, then eased down off the padded stool. The movement tugged her short skirt high on her pale thighs. She tugged at the hem on her way across the sales floor to the adjacent consulting room.

She brushed past the curtain hanging over the door and flipped on the lights. The air had gone smoky from the incense. She ignored the fragrant haze and crossed to the tarot table, where she began to clear her props away—a small bundle of sage in an abalone dish for smudging the cards between readings, and her layout scarves and tarot deck. Elise put the cards in a little wooden box she used to store them and had just turned her back when she heard the click of the light switch. The room went dark save for the dancing candle flames.

Her stomach clenched at the unexpected darkness. She glanced over her shoulder and saw Trip had come into the room. He pulled the silky curtains shut over the doorway.

"What are you doing?"

Rather than answer her, he gave her a roguish grin and started across the room to her. She put the wooden tarot box on the curio shelf to get it out of her hands, but before she could turn around again, Trip came up behind her and wrapped his tattooed arms around her waist, enveloping her in warmth and strength. "Does this answer your question?"

The smells of the hand-dipped incense he had been sorting into the display bins earlier in the day clung to him, and when he brushed her long red hair over to one side and kissed her neck, her ear, she bit her lip to control her smile. It didn't work.

His fringy black hair, razor-cut and soft as a feather, tickled her skin. He pinned her hips and rubbed his denim-clad erection back and forth across her ass. "What do you think I'm doing now?"

"Mmm...I don't know, but it feels promising."

He pushed up her skirt, exposing her nearly bare bottom to the cool air. A warm hand groped her right asscheek, rubbed and squeezed, and then he pulled away and gave her bottom a smart slap with an open hand. "You know," he said against her ear. "I don't think we've properly initiated this room."

The consultation room was probably the only room they hadn't fucked in. The day the Realtor had handed over the keys to the building, they had *initiated* the sales floor, and the window seat in the upstairs apartment.

Smiling at the memory, she arched her back against him. His cock fit perfectly against the crack of her ass. She wiggled her bottom against him. "So let me get this straight. You want to initiate this room, right now. During business hours?"

"Let's see, we've got no customers, shit weather, and I have the option of fucking you on the floor. Hmm. Sounds like a good idea to me." He tugged at the T-strap of her lace thong. "Want me to consult the spirits about it to be sure?"

She heard the smile in his voice and tsked at him for teasing her, although she secretly loved it. He picked up the antique black cat figurine with the oracle ball centered on its head like a third eye, and shook it.

"So let's have it, spirits. What do you say? A quickie in the tarot room to liven up the day—that sound like a good idea to you?" He stopped shaking the cat figurine. The little die wobbled inside the water-filled orb, and after a second or two, a message appeared in the tiny window. *Signs point to yes.*

"See?" He showed Elise the answer. "The pussy never lies." He put the cat back on the shelf. His hands found her breasts and cupped them, squeezed them through her T-shirt. "Who knows, if we did this with people here, we might actually get more customers."

She laughed at that, even as she leaned into him. Lack of customers or not, they were living their dream—a business in the French Quarter with an apartment upstairs. They could fuck till dawn, have breakfast in bed and still have time to walk downstairs and open the shop in the morning. When Trip slid both his hands beneath her blouse, her amusement faded into something more languorous and heady.

He found the underwire of her padded bra and pushed it upward, so the cups rested just above her breasts. Those eager hands cupped the small mounds and gently squeezed, his fingers brushing over her erect nipples.

"Mmm..." Her eyes slipped closed.

He nibbled the shell of her ear, and goose bumps broke out across her skin. Elise shivered and opened her eyes a fraction, glancing toward the large oval mirror on the wall, which reflected the curtained doorway.

The sound of his sharp breathing against the slope of her shoulder and the rough kiss of his lips against the back of her neck had her sighing. Her heart kicked against her ribs. Elise could barely think straight, but she remembered the time and the front door. She leaned her head back, against him. "You, um, locked the front door?"

He kissed the corner of her mouth. "No."

"Aren't you worried someone might walk in on us?"

"If they do, we'll tell them to pull up a chair and wait." Focused, he tugged at her thong and managed to work the scrap of lace down to the tops of her thighs. "Take this off."

"Yes, sir." Amused, she slipped the thong and her skirt down her long legs and kicked them aside, welcoming the cool kiss of air against her bare pussy.

When she stood facing him in nothing but her heels and her gauzy blouse, Trip touched his hand to the side of her face and lowered his mouth to hers.

Tongues twined, probed, rubbed against one another in a greedy kiss that left them both breathless. Elise moaned against his mouth, practically squirming with the need to feel him inside her. Rough fingers trailed down her body to the heat between her thighs. He stroked the soft folds of her pussy, delved deep to tease her, and then he found her clit with his thumb and began to rub the swollen bud in slow, tantalizing circles.

A tingling sensation raced through her from head to toe. Elise braced herself against the edge of the curio cabinet and widened her stance, welcoming his slow exploration. Watching her with heavy-lidded eyes, Trip went down on one knee and gently pulled her leg over his left shoulder.

She bit her lip as he nipped a path along her inner thigh. Sensitized to his touch, her stomach muscles jumped and twitched. He stroked his tongue along her slit, then pulled back to watch the sight of his slick fingers probing, sliding deep into her cunt. Her breath caught in her lungs. The friction was almost too intense to bear. Trip flicked his tongue against her clit, testing her before he settled his mouth over her and began to suck at her swollen bud. Moaning softly, Elise leaned her head back against the cabinet. It took every bit of willpower she had to keep from grinding her pussy against his face.

He kept her on the edge, fucking her with his fingers, teasing her clit with his tongue until Elise's legs trembled. She was so close to coming, the tension vibrated through her, building up.

She gasped for breath, more than ready to let it loose. Instead, he pulled away from her.

"Trip..." She whimpered his name in frustration.

His eyes were sympathetic. "Hold it back, baby. Don't come just yet."

He moved her leg from his shoulder carefully so she didn't stumble, then stood up and reached for the zipper of his jeans. His hard cock sprang forward, thick and ready. Elise captured the silky length in her hand. The dusting of dark hair from his navel to his balls rasped against her knuckles as she slowly stroked him. Trip raked his teeth over his lower lip and thrust into her fist. "I want to fuck your mouth."

The words made her womb clench. Elise went down on her knees in front of him, frustrated and more than willing to give him a sweet taste of his own medicine. She kissed the glistening eye of his cock, then flicked the head with her tongue before taking him slowly into her mouth.

Her blue eyes gazed up at him as she rolled her tongue around the head of his cock, tongue darting and flicking, drawing a hissing sound from between his clenched teeth. A smile beamed inside her at the intense look on his face. She could tell he was holding on, doing everything to make the moment last. She cupped his balls, massaging gently while sucking him deep to the back of her throat. Trip's stomach muscles clenched, and his hands tangled in her hair. "Oh, fuck yes, like that." He thrust between her lips and held himself there for a long minute before releasing her.

The wet smacking sounds and the hot look in his eyes urged her on, along with the thrilling awareness that at any moment, someone could walk into the shop and potentially catch them in the act. Her jaw held tense, she focused on sucking him in a slow, methodical rhythm that soon had him squirming. When his hips twitched involuntarily, Elise knew he was close to coming.

Barely a moment later, Trip groaned and pulled away from her, his breathing quick, his face bent in a scowl of determination. Eyes closed, he held himself very still, a hand cupped over his cock. "Fuckity fuck," he gritted through clenched teeth.

A wicked smile curved Elise's mouth.

After a long minute, he eased down onto the floor beside her and stretched out on his back. "I hope you're ready for me."

"More than ready," she promised, and glanced once toward the doorway, listening, while Trip lifted his hips and tugged his jeans down to his knees.

He held out a hand to her. "Come here."

The patterned carpet abraded her knees as she crawled closer. Elise smiled to herself. What was a little rug burn at a time like this? She straddled him, and with a hand braced on either side of his body, she leaned forward and rubbed her clit against his cock before he took his hard length in his fist and angled it upward. The head of his cock probed her slick entrance, and she shifted her hips, lifted them higher. Trip trembled beneath her. He was practically panting by the time he squeezed into her tight hole.

Elise wiggled down on him, and he uttered a curse under his breath. Hard hands gripped her hips, and he thrust home in a single solid movement. "Ah, yes!"

She stiffened, gasping at the sudden, deep penetration. A tingling sensation blossomed in the core of her stomach and rippled through her, prickling her skin. Her nipples tightened. Her clit throbbed. She hung her head and savored the fullness of his cock thrust fully inside her. A low moan left her lips and she began to move. Her pussy pulsed around his shaft. Elise shook her head, and somehow she found her voice. "Trip, oh god, fuck me. Fuck me hard. I need to come."

He hissed through clenched teeth. Hard hands gripped her hips and dragged her forward, pushed her back. Her hips bucked in a steady rhythm, grinding him. "That's it, baby. Ride my cock."

Shaking, she braced her hands on the firm wall of his chest. Her inner walls throbbed with each stabbing thrust. Her juices soaked him. Bodies tense and slick with sweat, they glided together, slow at first, and then faster.

Around them, the candles flickered in a sensual dance. Smoke from the incense curled up from the burners in thick ribbons and dissipated in the air, settling around the room into a silvery haze. A strawberry-scented fog.

On the edge, Elise sat straighter and shook her hair back over her shoulders. Their harsh breathing sounded loud in the silence of the room. Her swollen clit throbbed, aching for attention. Poised on the edge, she pushed Trip's hand aside and rubbed herself while he watched her with hooded fascination. She glided on his cock and strummed her clit with steady fingers that quickly pushed her past that threshold of pleasure.

The smoke seemed to drift through her, a ghost of lust that wrapped around her brain and seeped into her lungs, awakening a sweet, familiar tension inside her. Craving climax, she rolled her hips, meeting his sharp thrusts. A cool sweat broke out over her body when from somewhere inside her, a wave of pleasure spread through her like a winter chill. She came hard. Her breath hitched in her lungs as she shuddered over him, her body shaking, her cunt fluttering soft as butterfly wings around his cock.

Trip made a garbled sound low in his throat and buried himself to the hilt in her clutching pussy. When she stopped shaking, Elise squeezed her inner walls around him. His head dropped back, and his eyes closed. Muttering a curse under his breath, he clamped her hips tight against him and came.

Heart still racing, Elise bit back a smile and leaned down to kiss his chin. "I guess we've left our mark on this room."

Trip chuckled. "The spirits are pleased." He stroked his hands over her body and pulled her down beside him. They lay there, basking in the afterglow until the air grew cool, and the bells on the front door chimed.

Elise stiffened in alarm. Someone was moving around in the next room. She sat up abruptly and began grabbing for her clothes.

"Hello?" a man's voice called from the sales floor.

Trip caught her arm. "Don't panic. I got this." He gave her a quick kiss and staggered to his feet. "Be right there!" he called out to whoever had come into the shop. He quickly pulled up his jeans and tucked in his semi-hard cock before zipping his fly.

"I'll lock up after this guy leaves," he told her on his way across the room. "It's about closing time anyway." He pushed through the curtains, and a second later, Elise heard him greet whoever was shopping out front.

She pulled on her skirt and grabbed a box of tissues off the little magazine table in the corner. Trip's come trickled down to slick her inner thighs. She stood by the wastebasket and cleaned herself up before pulling on her panties, aware that she still needed to blow out all the candles and snuff the burning incense. She didn't mind one bit. A smile curved her lips. Her tarot client hadn't shown up, but setting up the consultation room certainly hadn't been a waste.

FIVE P.M.
SOMEWHERE

Kristina Lloyd

I heard the silence at dawn and knew we were trapped. Beyond the windows, an eerie, deadened calm smothered the world, and no birds sang. Ordinarily, the countryside's quiet is expansive. You can hear the space, can sense sky and far-off hills in a landscape teeming with tiny life. The morning was echoless and flat. When I peeped through the frilly bedroom curtains, the village square had gone, reshaped by a thick padding of snow, heavy flakes falling fast in the muted silver light.

My first thought: *How pretty.* My second: *He forgot the fucking gin.*

I hurried back to bed, feet like ice, and recalled my cousin, Mel, comparing the taste of gin to sucking on a Christmas tree. Well, we had a tree downstairs, pine needles glittering with tinsel, but I could think of more enticing objects to suck on. But then I wasn't sure he deserved it since he'd failed so spectacularly in his gin duty.

Next to me, Brynn grunted in his sleep, his feet flinching

from mine as I sought out his body warmth.

No gin. Given that gin was the key ingredient in the dirty martinis scheduled for three o'clock, our lack presented us with a problem.

At three, there wasn't a cocktail in sight although the two of us were extremely well chilled. Brynn was trying to dig out the car with a spade he'd found in the lean-to while I was using a metal tea tray, pocked with corrosion, to scoop and flip snow to the edge of the small courtyard. The tray was decorated with an antique picture of London's Natural History Museum, dandies on horseback milling about in front of the grand building. I wondered how the tray had ended up in an old stone cottage over two hundred miles north. What was its story? Holiday lets are strange places, personal possessions popping up unexpectedly in a contrived but welcoming domesticity. Hoping vainly someone had left behind a personal possession of gin, we'd checked every cupboard, but no such luck.

"I think we should quit," said Brynn, straightening. He shoved his spade in a bank of snow, sniffed and touched his nose with the back of his glove. His beanie cap was pulled down low, his face bright and flushed, his breath clouding in the air. "Temperature's dropping. It's going to freeze tonight. Essential journeys only. And however much you like a tipple, gin isn't essential."

"Essential to a martini," I countered. I looked up at him, this dark-hatted man framed by a white sky, snow-clad mountains at his shoulders, and I thought how our surroundings, stark and sparkling with frost, had the icy clarity of a gin martini. It made me long to sip perfection. Some people choose hot toddies in winter, but on a cold day I prefer the bite of a cold drink.

"It's only a drink."

Kneeling, I resumed flipping snow aside with the tray. "It's not *only* a drink," I said. "It's our anniversary tradition."

"Then fuck it. Let's break with tradition, celebrate some other way."

"I'm superstitious."

"No, you're not," said Brynn. "You're trying to guilt-trip me. I've already apologized, so can we please move on?" He tugged his spade free and began stomping toward the house, compacted snow creaking beneath his boots.

"It wasn't hard, though, was it?" I called. "We load up the car. I sort out the food, you sort out the drinks. And the one thing you forget—"

He spun around. "The phone rang! I got distracted. For chrissakes, let it drop, will you?"

He went indoors and I listened to him stamping his feet on the rear porch, unzipping his jacket. I wanted to be indoors too, warm and dry. He was right, I was being unreasonable. The trouble was, throughout our relationship, I'd always felt our anniversary was something I organized and valued with Brynn hopping on for the ride. If I didn't put the effort in, our special day would sail past, unacknowledged. I view anniversaries as reminders not to take each other for granted. Admittedly, Brynn had been making more of an effort these last couple of years, but him forgetting my gin at the last minute seemed to encapsulate the problem of his noncommittal approach to mutual appreciation. And he'd managed to remember the whiskey for his sour, hadn't he?

I stood and dusted down my damp knees. Indoors, Brynn was sat at the table in the overly floral kitchen, drinking tea and reading a magazine that didn't look like his kind of thing at all. The pages showed pictures of fields and fences rather than software. He hadn't made tea for me. In the living room, I lit the imitation log fire and warmed my hands before its leaping flames. In the kitchen, Brynn turned pages, loudly.

I wondered where in the world it was five o'clock. Not here, that's for sure, even though, literally, it almost was. Extraordinary to think that six years ago, on the day we first hooked up, it had been a mild December afternoon, buildings blurred and sparkling with low golden sunshine. I'd taken a day's leave and was in town for some leisurely Christmas shopping when I bumped into him. He was the new guy at work, employed on a temporary, part-time contract to assist in the company's website overhaul. We'd spoken a few times, nothing more than that. Watercooler. Cute guy. Friendly. No wedding ring (just checking).

"Do you fancy a drink?" he asked.

"Now?"

"No problem if you're busy."

I checked my watch. "It's three o'clock." My tone must have implied, quite accurately, I thought this was too early in the day to drink.

"C'mon, you know what they say. It's always five o'clock somewhere."

And that's how we ended up in a quiet cocktail bar in the middle of a Thursday afternoon poring over a menu of extravagant, frivolous beverages.

After some deliberation, Brynn chose a whiskey sour. I closed the menu. I hadn't needed to look. "Dirty martini, three olives, gin not vodka, stirred not shaken."

"Seems you're a woman who knows what she wants," he said, apparently impressed.

"Yup. And I aim to get it."

Initially, that was an asset as far as Brynn was concerned. He never had to second-guess me. A few years later, it was a failing. I was inflexible, a perfectionist, a woman unable to go with the flow.

Well, I was determined to go with the flow of being snow-bound, our regular plans to recreate our first drink scuppered by one small moment of forgetfulness. It was no big deal. We could do something else instead. Watch TV, play Scrabble, have a row.

Outside, the afternoon was dark. Snow shimmered in the lamplight of the buried village. A couple trudged across the square, knees high as they marched in slow motion, heads down. Brynn began moving about in the kitchen.

I went to tell him I was taking a bath to warm up. He stood by the open fridge, giving me an effortful smile. "Can I join you in a while?" he asked.

Ah, so we were calling a truce, or trying to. "Sure," I said. "That'd be nice."

I felt myself thawing out in the bath, physically and emotionally. I recalled how, weeks after our first cocktail, when we were excitable and loved-up, Brynn had written me a wonderfully romantic email name-checking cities that had been in the five p.m. time zone when we'd sat down for cocktails: Helsinki, Kiev, Istanbul, Beirut, Cairo, Cape Town. But, he declared, the only place he'd wanted to be was with me in a bar in Bromley.

Would he say the same thing now? Given my grouchiness, I could hardly blame him if he'd prefer Beirut. I was a romantic and a control freak, that was my problem. I got fixated on an ideal version of events and when life didn't go as planned, I felt cheated. On the plus side, Brynn's more laid-back approach counterbalanced my rigidity. Our differences made us a great team—and a terrible one.

I soaked for a while, mulling things over. Brynn didn't appear. I wondered if he'd fallen asleep in front of the fire like an old man. *Well, if he has*, I told myself, *that's fine. Go with the flow.* I was about to step out of the bath when I heard his footsteps on the stairs.

"You ready?" he called. Enthusiasm twinkled in his voice.

I was weak with heat from the water but curiosity perked me up. "For what?"

Brynn strode into the bathroom and took a large towel from where it was warming on a rail. "It's cocktail hour," he declared. "And I'm about to make the world's first alcohol-free dirty martini, no glasses required." He gave a small bow, bath towel draped waiter-style over his arm. "Mr. Mixologist at your service. Now, if you wouldn't mind stepping out of the water..."

Laughing, I did as instructed. Brynn quickly wrapped me in the towel and a tight embrace, rubbing vigorously at my arms and back. "Dry," he said. "Because a dirty martini needs dry vermouth."

I couldn't remember the last time someone had dried me. The cotton on my skin, thick, brisk and absorbent, was both invigorating and comforting. Brynn took care to towel me all over, making me laugh hard when he knelt at my feet to dry my toes individually.

"It tickles," I gasped, thinking how different it is when someone does something to you that you'd ordinarily do yourself.

He dried my legs, making me feel tall and strong as his hands rose higher, the towel lightly scouring my skin. I soon stopped laughing. When he rubbed at the folds between my thighs, my groin pulsed softly, similar to the tickle mechanism sparked by another's touch. He stood, reaching behind me to dry the split of my buttocks. He rose higher, shifting the towel to find dry patches as he glided into the crease beneath each breast, nudged into my armpits and wiped the curve behind my ears.

"Dry?" he asked.

"Very," I replied then added, smiling, "Well, not quite."

Brynn smiled too, catching my drift as he tucked the towel

around me. "The ice is outside," he said, "and I reckon we've had enough of that today. Pre-chilled glasses. That's what we made earlier. Too much ice dilutes the gin. Not good."

He edged me back against the aqua green wall, lips teasing mine with fleeting kisses. Pressing me lightly in place, he leaned away to tug his jumper over his head. His dark hair went wonky with static and he returned to kissing me, his face taking on that loose, serious look it does when he's aroused. He kissed a track toward my ear.

"You're all clean and pure," he said. "And I'm dirty, unwashed."

He slid a hand into my towel, cupping my waist, his thumb skimming below my breasts. My skin tingled and his unshaven jaw scratched my neck. I reached for his swollen groin, understanding that our lovemaking was somehow to be a dirty martini made flesh.

As I slipped into the softness of lust and Brynn stepped out of his jeans, I ran through the ingredients: chilled glasses, gin, dry vermouth, olives, brine, and someone to stir not shake it. Well, this certainly was high-concept sex. I hadn't a clue how Brynn was going to pull it off.

He moved toward me again, his cock rising thick and hard. I nodded at his groin. "That your swizzle stick?"

Brynn laughed. "Might be, yes. But first I need something to swizzle." He untucked my towel and the cotton fell to a heap at my feet, leaving me naked against the bathroom wall. "Correct me if I'm wrong," he continued, "but dry vermouth is French, no?"

I arched my back, wanting his touch, trying to recall who'd said the perfect martini is a glass of gin waved in the direction of Italy. That is, low on the vermouth. Italy or France? Clearly, I hadn't been paying attention to my vermouths. Brynn said, "French means French kissing," and he ground against me, running gentle kisses over my lips before flicking his tongue deeper, our mouths opening to explore in a manner we no longer practiced, yielding to the passion of the moment rather than going through the motions.

Brynn cupped my vulva where I was swollen and warm. Drawing away, rubbing me gently, he said, "And a splash of *soixante-neuf*." He sank to his knees on the thick carpet, pulling me down to join him in the narrow space between bath and wall. We moved as if choreographed, years of domestic and sexual cooperation allowing us to harmonize our bodies effortlessly as we occupied a new space.

Brynn lapped at my wet split and I took the bulky head of his cock into my mouth. Had I been convinced vermouth was made in China, I wouldn't have challenged this incorporation of French delicacies. Strange, but although we'd been in that position a thousand times before, with our mouths moist and full, the unfamiliarity of our surroundings brought a fresh charge to the exchange. Brynn's tongue darted around my clit as it always does, rubbing more steadily on the right side as he always does. And when I was close, he curled his fingers inside me, pressing, pulling, easing his cock from my mouth so I could gasp and focus on receiving, not giving. And then I was coming in the warm, misty bathroom, coming over and over because I was miles away from home and from my ordinary self.

Brynn maneuvered into the space between my thighs, his hand gliding lightly over my belly as I dropped down from my peak. "Turn over," he said.

Feeling blissfully floppy, I got onto my hands and knees, thinking he would fuck me, climax and we'd be done. I underestimated him.

"Three olives," he said.

I yowled in pain as he sank his teeth into the flesh of one buttock. It hurt. It really, sodding hurt, and I'd been in such a pleasant, post-orgasmic haze. "Bastard," I hissed as the pain spiked. He released me. The pain kept rising; then, just as it was abating, Brynn bit into a fresh patch of flesh, holding his teeth tightly in place. "Ah, ah, ah!" I cried. When I was on the verge of swinging around to hit him, he released me. The fiery pain soared. Then, without giving me chance to feel the heat subside, he went vampiric on another piece of cheek.

"No more! Stop!" I cried. And I meant it. I didn't like the pain. And yet I liked that Brynn was inflicting it, liked that he was running the show and I was at the mercy of his imagination and desire. Our glasses were chilled, we'd had vermouth and now three sharp, vicious olives. "The gin had better be good," I growled, twisting around to him, "because that fucking hurt."

Brynn laughed. "Only the best gin for you. Step this way, ma'am." He helped me to my feet, a hand caressing my tender arse, and led me from bathroom to bedroom. "Close your eyes," he said.

Before doing so, I caught a glimpse of the bedroom with its drawn chintz curtains and half tester bed rising grandly against the floral walls. Flames danced in the black lead fireplace, casting the room in a fluttering, amber glow. I saw nothing that might stand as a gin substitute. I allowed Brynn to guide me into the warm room, keeping my eyes shut as I giggled and shuffled toward the bed. Following Brynn's orders, I lay on the soft bed, fighting the urge to open my eyes at the squeaky sound of a plastic packet being opened.

"What are you doing?" I said. "You're making me nervous."

Brynn responded by placing a strip of something cold and clammy across my stomach. I tensed fractionally. He lay another over my breast, draping a cool weight over my nipple, making me shiver. I smelled fish. "What's that?" I asked. "It's not the smoked salmon, is it?" I remembered how I'd packed it for the anniversary breakfast we'd postponed in favor of checking weather reports and shoveling snow.

"Open wide," said Brynn. A thin sliver of flesh touched my tongue, folding into my mouth like damp silk, its sea-salty richness and smoky undertone making my taste buds tingle. In my darkness, I ate, the salmon's softness melting into quick-splitting fragments.

"Salmon smoked over juniper and beech," said Brynn. "Juniper for gin."

"Very clever," I murmured as Brynn brought another morsel to my lips. The salmon flowed onto my tongue, a liquefaction of sparkling Scottish lochs, leaping muscle, subtle sweetness and woodfire. As I ate, so did Brynn, his stubble catching on my skin as he bent to lift flesh from my flesh. For a brief, thrilling moment, I felt as if he were consuming me; as if I were surrendering my body to him in the most literal of ways.

A hard flood of eroticism pulsed in my cunt, making my tissues pouch to swollen, heaving fullness. Between my thighs, I was moist and succulent, my flesh as salt-sweet as the salmon. When Brynn dipped his head there, tongue delving and lapping, another orgasm began to bunch inside me, ripples tightening. I opened my eyes, hips rocking in search of a stronger touch. Brynn withdrew, hooked his hands under my thighs and jerked me closer. He ran his cock over my wetness, making me whimper with want. Pushing my legs back and wide, he nudged at my entrance, then sank into me with slow control.

His pace was steady as he plunged in and out before shifting his angle, pushing my legs further back. He locked onto a spot that made us both groan and, staying there, he drove harder and faster until we'd worn the sensation away. Then he flipped me onto all fours, quickly finding another hot spot as he rammed hard and deep. Then I was sideways with my leg on his shoulder, then I was straddling him and then I wasn't. On my hands and knees again, I rubbed my clit as Brynn slammed with rising ferocity, his cries peaking. His cock swelled inside me, then he held deep, body twitching as he came. Moments later, I joined him, fireworks popping behind my eyes as Brynn's blissful cries echoed in my ears.

When we parted, we lay together in a strong embrace. "And that," said Brynn, sounding as if he'd just done an hour at the gym, "was your shot of olive brine."

I laughed. "Dirtiest martini I ever had. My compliments to the bartender."

Brynn mussed idly at my hair. "Mmm."

I nuzzled at his chest, tasting his sweat on my lips. "You're all salty," I said approvingly.

After a while, Brynn said, "Key ingredient to margarita. Salt."

I stroked his chest. "Ah, but no tequila in the house."

Brynn shrugged. "We could improvise."

"I like this bar," I said. "I could stay here all night."

"Getting hammered!" added Brynn, laughing.

And so we did stay there all night, mixing our drinks like there was no tomorrow while outside, the world froze around us in slow, crystalline crackles.

Days later, back to work and reality, I was left with faded bruises on my butt. My skin was dotted with three neat circles, green like the olives in my imagined drink. I checked them when I dressed, when I went to the bathroom and when I showered. Those three bruises were a reminder that if you want it to be, it's always five o'clock somewhere.

SIX P.M. THE AFTER-DINNER HOUR

Sommer Marsden

I want sugar," I whispered.

We had just cleared our dinner plates. We were eating Paleo. It was awesome. You know, except for the no sugar part.

"No sugar," Mark said.

"A little sugar."

"You can have honey candy," he said. And he smiled. I hated honey and he knew it.

"You are enjoying this."

"I do admit," he said, tracing a line down my chest, "that it's fun to see you squirm."

I did feel a bit crawly. Day three of kicking sugar always gets me. "I'm going through withdrawal," I gasped. It would have been funny but it was true.

"There's that coconut oil—"

"Bleh with the coconut oil," I said. I was snapping my fingers. I needed a distraction. "I need to...*do* something," I said. "Why is this bothering me so much?"

"Day three always gets you, Annie."

"Hmph."

"Clever retort."

I grabbed him by his flannel shirt and crushed against him. "Kiss me."

"Maybe I need to be wooed."

"Kiss me!"

"It's only six p.m.," Mark said, his voice teasing. But his hands were palming my ass and I felt a spear of arousal right up the center of me. "Proper people do not fu—"

I kissed him quiet, pouring all my sugar lust into that kiss.

"I'm not proper," I said. I curled my fingers to his cock and squeezed.

Somehow, Mark kept his face straight. "We retire for a beverage on the veranda during the after-dinner hour," he said. But there was a slight hint of grit in his voice.

"I need something more in my after-dinner hour," I said and squeezed again.

"Sorry. You're out of luck, you'll have to wait until we've retired for the night. Until the shades are drawn and the door is locked and the lights are ou—"

I kissed him again, smashing my curves to his lean lines. I felt the hump of his cock ride the split of my sex through my thin cashmere leggings. I felt the pound of his heart against my breast as I curled my fingers in his hair and yanked just a bit. My pussy went warm and fluid for him then. If I couldn't have my sugar, I wanted my *sugar.*

He started to speak, his big hands splaying my hips. I threw myself into the kiss even more and ended up biting him. Mark started, his big body going stiff under mine, and then he growled. He'd only made that sound a few times—ever—and it raised the fine hairs on my neck when he did.

"Annie," he said. His green eyes had gone darker. More the color of moss now than grass.

"Sorry," I said, but a small curl of anxiety filled my gut.

He wiped a finger over his mouth and held it out to me. Blood.

"I didn't mean to—"

It had all shifted so quickly and my heart was a runaway thing in my chest. Mark walked from the room and I waited. I heard him sit on our big crème-colored sofa and then softly, "Come here, Annie."

I wondered as I walked in there, my brightly colored turquoise and red silk tunic whispering around my thighs, if I'd done it on purpose. If I'd bitten him for this reason.

"Yes?" I stood in a classic ballet position. My toes pointed outward, my knees not quite locked.

Mark patted his lap. "Don't pretend you don't know."

We rarely went here. It was usually when we were both craving something...*more*. More than just fun sex or making love or a quick, amusing fuck. And usually there was a trigger. And it...worked. God, how it worked.

Bloodletting, I thought wildly. Bloodletting had been the trigger this time.

Then I had Concrete Blonde in my head as I made my way forward on nervous feet.

"I—" I stopped. What was I going to say? There was nothing to say. I noticed my hands were shaking and it felt like my stomach was keeping time. A fine tremble worked through all of me so I felt like a tuning fork, vibrating with some magical musical tone.

He patted again once I was standing in front of him and I went to kneel, but Mark held up a hand to stop me. "Ah-ah. I think you need to ditch the dress thing."

"Tunic," I corrected before I thought better of it.

His dark eyes found mine and they were harder than normal.

Flatter than normal. Not as warm. The eyes of a man who made me pay for my transgressions. "Pardon?"

"I mean...yes. Okay." I gathered the soft fabric in my hand and relished the smoothness of the colorful garb. When I yanked it over my head, my hair rustled softly around my head, tickling my cheeks, covering my eyes. All of my senses were heightened from the rush of adrenaline and bursts of fear.

He held his hand out and for a second I was confused and then I gave him the tunic, his big fist compacting the silk like it was nothing more than tissue paper. He patted my ass and I flinched as if he'd struck a blow, but my cunt then pulsed wetly for the same reason.

"Let's just get these out of the way, then, too," he said.

I pushed the leggings down and his hand instantly cupped my bottom. A proprietary touch that made goose bumps race along my lower back, down my flanks. My pussy felt plump and slick, my heart out of control.

"Now get down here."

I lowered myself on shaking legs and draped myself across his lap. Wondering how I looked, if I looked beautiful—I hoped I looked beautiful. Nervous was fine as long as there was beauty involved.

His finger dove beneath the elastic of my panty leg and into me. My back bowed seemingly on its own, my breath rushing free of me. My mind narrowed down to my need. And that first blow...how I ached for it.

Over his lap, I tried to suck in enough air to banish the spots in my eyes.

His hands smoothed up from mid-thigh, stroked my ass and then back down. Mark did that over and over until I was soothed and feeling boneless. Conversationally, he said, "Missing that sugar now?"

"No," I breathed.

He's very good. He had me fooled. I was damn near hanging limp over his lap when the first crack came. A blow that split the silence in the room like an axe and made my head snap back from the rush.

"One," he said softly and laughed. He had never made me count. I doubted he ever would. He always gave me eight and that was that. His lucky number. And then he fucked me until I damn near wept.

I tried to shift to relieve the heated blush of pain in my bottom, but his finger tugged the waistband of my panties and he tsked at me. "Where you going, baby?"

The second blow landed across the first. A blazing X on my ass that in my mind's eye burned like a ring of fire.

I figured he'd switch then. Go for the opposite cheek. Instead, he peeled back my pale yellow panties and laid a stripe of molten lava along the already sensitive skin.

I yelped, tears wetting my eyes. But my pussy...oh, things were wet there, too. But not in a bad way. In a positively maddening way. I assured myself I could take it, I could take it *all*, because what he'd do to me when all was said and done would make the fierce bite of each blow a distant memory. Only the throbbing remainder would matter to me soon.

Soon.

Four was a broad stripe right below my asscheek, and it startled me. He'd never gone that low or triggered that many sparkles of pain. I gasped. Halfway there, I reassured myself.

The next one came. "Five." Mark laughed, but his hand barely came down on the untouched side of my ass. I flinched but for no reason. The touch was almost a caress. "Oh, so skittish," he tutted.

I blushed. Feeling silly. I had flinched before I needed to and when he touched me a rich rush of fluid had come out of me. There would be no hiding that from him. Even as I thought it, he slipped a finger into the crotch of my panties. He chuckled and I blushed harder.

I was so preoccupied I forgot to pay attention, and blow six was definitely not a caress. It was an ear-cracking blow that had me dancing over his lap. I pressed my knees together, my lips, my thighs, hoping the pressure would take the bite out of the pain.

It did not.

Mark gave up the premise and pushed my panties down. "So, so wet. I doubt a gummy candy or a bonbon would have done *this* for you. Do you think?"

I shook my head.

He pushed a finger into me. The wet sound that accompanied his penetration made me hang my head but I sighed with pleasure when I did it. A second finger joined the first and a wet pulse of gratification came next.

"You are very wet, Annie. Were you aware?"

I nodded.

His free hand struck me. It was a thudding blow that rattled my teeth for a moment.

"I didn't catch that?" he said good-naturedly. At least he *sounded* good-natured.

"Yes," I said.

Mark pulled his fingers free, his hand smoothing over my lower back, teasing gooseflesh up in its wake. He softly stroked the swell of each cheek and then lower, to the tender untouched places just below. I knew that seven and eight were coming. I knew it and I could not fix my mind on anything else. It was all my mind could grasp.

Panic rose in my chest and stalled my breathing.

"Yes, what?" he cooed to me.

"Yes, I was aware."

He grunted but as my reward for keeping my mind on track, he slipped his fingers back into my body. Shoving them deep he nudged me in the place that made my throat tickle and my cunt flutter. I was going to come soon—whether from plain or pleasure or just promise, I didn't know. And I didn't care.

"Are you ready?"

I didn't say anything. He surprised me by pinching the tender skin that had already been plumped up by blows.

"Ready for what?" I gasped.

"The last two?"

I nodded, caught myself, made myself say it aloud. "Yes."

"Hard or soft?"

Again he'd caught me off guard. Hard or soft? Hard or soft? They were two entirely different sensations. Two entirely different reactions. One was no better than the other. One was hard to take but the payoff was exquisite. One was easier to take and the pleasure was still ample, but different.

"Hard," I said without thinking.

He laughed. The laugh unnerved me but he said "Very well" and then I felt him stiffen just a bit. My body followed suit, going rigid the way I would if I could see my car about to crash. Which is, ironically, the worst possible thing to do. And it was in this instance, too, because I tensed all of myself—preparing, I thought, for a fierce strike. What came was a whispering kiss of palm on flesh. He barely touched me, and I think I shocked us both when I burst into tears.

The rush of adrenaline and mental preparation left me bewildered and in a semi-state of shock when nothing like I was anticipating happened. Emotion overload was the result and I found myself draped over his lap, sobbing like a lunatic.

Mark laughed in that way he does that says I am crazy but he loves me. Another butterfly of a kiss on my bottom as his palm barely came down again and he muttered, "Eight."

And then he was moving me, tugging me, rearranging me—and me feeling foolish and spent and damn near boneless. "Come up here, Annie."

He got me on his lap, facing him, and then I watched my fingers as if they were not mine, working his button and yanking his zipper to get him bare. My pussy so wet and swollen I felt full though I wasn't. Beyond ready. Pretty much desperate.

"Good girl," he said softly, kissing my throat. I leaned in, still confused—feeling a bit empty like a husk from all the weeping—and feeling a bit ditzy.

His lips found my collarbone and then his teeth scraped me as he gripped my hips and positioned the head of his cock—flushed and hard and silken smooth at the tip—along my slit. I lowered myself slowly, watching him watch me, feeling him study my tear-streaked face.

"All I wanted was some sugar," I said and smiled. The stupid feeling was waning, the good feeling from his cock in me expanding.

"This is better than sugar," he grunted, and thrust up hard. I gasped, letting him hold me by my hips and keep me where he needed.

Mark rotated and thrust just so until I was panting, and when he kissed me, swallowing those small puffs of air, he gripped me tight and thrust up hard. I came, still kissing his lips and grinding my hips down to meet him.

"One more," he said. "The after-dinner hour isn't done yet." One hand found my nipple and his fingers—so strong from manual labor all day in the sun—clamped down hard enough to make me hiss. But the pressure was sublime. Exactly what I needed to sharpen my mind and my arousal.

I was moving side to side in a mindless metronome motion, trying to grind my clit to his pubic bone. Rushing toward another orgasm at his command. His free hand kept me steady at the flare of my hips even as he continued the pressure on my nipple. His lips on my shoulder as soft as his fingers' grip was hard.

"Come for me once more, sweetheart."

His body was controlled chaos, his rhythm a frenzy. His breathing told the story, he was on the edge. And just when his eyes went darker and his face grew serious, I clenched myself up around him and he released my hip to land a final blow on the swell of my left cheek. It was a biting sudden pain that did everything I'd anticipated that undelivered blow would do.

A rush of heat, a bite of pain, a swell of blissful pleasure and I was coming, chanting his name like some deranged cheerleader. He released my nipple, and the blood rushing back into that tortured flesh only amped up my release.

I pressed my forehead to his and he roared out his climax, his stubble rasping against my cheek, his heart pounding under my palm splayed on his chest.

"Still miss sugar?" He tugged a hunk of my hair and kissed me.

I leaned into him and pressed my forehead to his chest. My thighs were still shaking, my body still cooling. "I'm pretty sure if we can replace it with *that*, I could go cold turkey."

"I plan to make you stick to it."

"Stick it to me, baby," I said. And meant it.

SEVEN P.M.
KINKY CRAFT
NIGHT

Teresa Noelle Roberts

I t looks like spiders threw a party in here. Tacky spiders on acid."

Sitting on the living room floor, where I'd been luxuriating in my piles of new yarn, I looked up at Jace, who'd been at the gym. He must have run home because he was still lightly sheened with sweat. Yum. "I scored at a yard sale this afternoon. All this"—I gestured at the yarn taking up most of the living room floor—"was just five dollars. Two big trash bags full, and some of it's great."

Jace picked up a huge skein of safety orange super-bulky acrylic, looking as though he thought it might bite. "Really?"

"That would be some of the not-so-great stuff." I laughed. "It must have been some elderly relative's whole stash: the good, the bad and the really, really ugly, complete with one each of four sizes of aluminum needles, which are already in the recycling bin because even I can't justify keeping unmatched knitting needles."

"You could already knit sweaters for everyone in Providence with the yarn you already have. Why get all this yarn you'll never use?"

"I couldn't help myself. Don't you know yarn's addictive? There's no such thing as too much." Jace grimaced. He got the slightly alarmed look of a man who realizes he's fallen in love with a Crazy Fiber-Arts Lady and might wake up buried alive in miscellaneous wool, cotton and acrylic, so I attempted to reassure him. "I'm not keeping all of it. I'm sorting it into keep, give to Mom for her charity knitters, and..." I gestured at the evil orange stuff in Jace's hand, which looked like it had been thrown up by a jack-o'-lantern. "I guess toss. It hurts to throw out yarn, but I can't imagine what else I'd do with some of this scary stuff. Or what anyone would, for that matter."

Jace pulled a length of the orange yarn out of its skein, tugged on it experimentally to gauge its strength. "I have a few ideas." He smiled slowly and evilly. "Don't throw this out yet."

Which led, around seven o'clock that evening, to me standing in the bedroom wearing a chest harness of that awful orange yarn. The yarn also bound my hands together behind my back, wrists to elbows. The remains of the skein formed a crotch binding. Where it rubbed my pussy lips, the yarn felt only slightly softer than Brillo. Normally, that's not a quality I like in a yarn, but under the circumstances, the slight discomfort added to the excitement at being tied up and played with, like I was suffering for Jace. Like I was being twisted and kinked like yarn was when it was knitted. The yarn, if it had a résumé, could add damp and smelling of horny girl to its list of dubious qualifications, along with screamingly bright, stiff, and made from long-dead dinosaurs. While I still had a few functional brain cells, I mentally noted to do a second sort of the yarn and make sure nothing this nasty texture was in the bag for

Mom's charity knitting circle. Chemo patients, preemie babies and homeless people had enough problems without hats apparently knit out of old pot scrubbers.

"How does that feel?" Jace ran two fingers between my legs, dipping into the moistness where the yarn held my lips open. I shivered under his caress, at the way it echoed from my pussy lips to my clit, from my clit to my nipples, and from my nipples up to the place in my brain that was starting to open up, so if all went well I'd soon be getting that floaty endorphin-rush feeling.

I was still clearheaded enough to answer Jace's question, though based on past experience I wouldn't be coherent much longer. "Hemp rope has nothing on cheap acrylic yarn for making me aware how tender my tender bits are."

He laughed. "And it's much easier to wash. We may be on to something." He raised his fingers, slick with my juices, to his lips, and licked sensuously, never taking his eyes from my rapt face.

I drew a deep, sharp breath, thrilling at the constriction of the yarn around my body.

Thrilling at the lust and love flaming in Jace's dark eyes.

Thrilling at the fabric of us, the way we were woven or knitted together into a wonderful creation.

While I was busy quivering, Jace grabbed another skein, this one a baby-weight acrylic in a weird yellowy-greenish-brown that I couldn't imagine on a baby, or on anyone else, for that matter.

He threaded one end through the ring on my left nipple and ran the yarn down my body to my navel piercing. Fire followed his touch and lingered where the yarn lay against my skin. This yarn was an unfortunate color, but lovely and soft. It teased at my nipple, at the skin of my belly. He drew the yarn down to the ring in my clit hood and threaded it through. As he moved up again to the belly ring, yarn snaked over my clit, tantalizing me until I was grinding against the air.

Finally, he pulled the yarn through my right nipple ring, forming a sensual spiderweb connecting all those sensitive areas, so one movement could tug on them all.

(Yeah, I knit and crochet and I have a bunch of body piercings and my boyfriend and I are kinky. Get over it. Fiber arts aren't just for little old ladies, and based on some of the conversations I've had at knitting workshops, not all little old ladies are as demure and vanilla as I used to assume. But I digress.)

When all my piercings were connected to his satisfaction, Jace grabbed the safety shears. There was a whole ugly skein unraveling on the floor next to us and he could have snicked the yarn without getting the shears anywhere near me. But what fun would that be?

The blades were just pleasantly cool on my heated skin—he hadn't pulled them out of the freezer this time. As he moved them over my nipples, I still shivered, clenched in something that danced on the border between dread and anticipation. I knew the scissors were blunt. That's kind of the reason for having EMT safety shears when you're tying someone up; cutting's only fun if you're doing it on purpose. But my nerve endings and the primitive part of my brain where the endorphins live didn't register the bluntness, only the cold kiss of metal on sensitive skin that covered important internal organs.

My knees weakened. My heart pounded. And when that cool metal kissed between my legs, so did my clit. I'd been wet before, but the shears came away dripping, leaving a trail of my own juices on my belly and breasts.

I closed my eyes as Jace opened the shears near my nipple, imagining delicious horrors, and when they snicked shut with

nothing more ominous than yarn caught between them, something exploded in my brain. By the time I could actually process
anything other than euphoria, Jace had tied the cut ends together
and was tugging outward.

Right nipple, left nipple, belly and clit. Each pull hit all four,
jolting me with pleasure and an intense awareness of the yarn
connecting them, of the hundreds of nerve endings connecting
them, of the time and love and lust connecting me and Jace,
joining us together into something greater, like yarn knotted
upon itself becomes a garment.

Bondage can be weirdly solitary, at least for me. When Jace
is painstakingly tying me up to immobilize me or decorate me
with rope (or in this case, hideous yarn), I get lost in sensation, so far in my own head and body I enter a meditative state,
intensely aware, yet detached—a kind of sexual Zen. Unfortu-
nately, I also detach from Jace.

That doesn't bother me at the time because not a lot is going
to bother me when my nerve endings and I are enjoying a flight
through inner space. But when Jace does something to bring that
connection back, like those little tugs on all my piercings, my
flight becomes even better because we're exploring the galaxy
together.

Keeping the tension on the yarn, Jace leaned in and kissed
me like rocket fuel. He'd taken his shirt off, and his skin felt
cool against mine, cool and delicious because I was feverish,
burning up inside with the pleasure of that very second, of his
big hand on my ass, the yarn keeping tension on my nipples and
hood, the strength of his body, his lips both soft and fervent,
his tongue assertive but not aggressive as it danced with mine.
He tasted faintly of cinnamon, but mostly he tasted like Jace. I
moaned into his mouth, pressed myself against him.

When his hand cracked down on my ass, I squealed and

jumped, but it was a squeal of delight, and I promptly stuck my butt out and wriggled it, hoping for more.

"You need a little pain, girl?"

Even though all connection between my brain and my lips seemed to be lost in space, I still blurted out an eager "Yes!"

Jace arranged me so my upper body was sprawled on the bed, my ass thrust out. With my arms tied behind me, I felt strain up the back of my legs, but it was a good strain, like what I felt in my arms from the bondage. The crotch rope pulled and teased at my cunt lips, and somehow—probably because Jace made sure of it—the yarn through my clit ring was caught up just enough under me for a slight, constant pressure.

He warmed me up with his hand, starting slow and light, each smack more like a love tap that warmed my butt without much sting. Each blow was a single stitch in something bigger, though; after a few dozen, my ass was getting sensitized. I felt Jace's hand more acutely, more pleasurably. I squirmed. Pressure from the yarn wrapping my pussy hit my clit, a direct jolt that made me gasp. The movement also reminded me of the way I was bound, of the way Jace embraced me through the yarn. Warmth spread through my whole body. "Now," I said, my voice barely audible even to me. "More, please."

He began to spank harder, hell and heaven at the same time. It stung, so I couldn't help trying to wriggle away, but the sting quickly morphed into heat, so I pushed my ass back out for more. Every movement, whether toward Jace's blows or away, made me more keenly aware of yarn around me, yarn through my piercings, yarn binding me.

Jace binding me.

Jace and I bound together.

The world narrowed to my body and his, his hand and my ass, his fiber art and my skin.

I ached with arousal, but at the same time I didn't need to come, wasn't begging and mewling for release. I was on a rocket trip through space, propelled by fossil fuel in the form of acrylic yarn, and the renewable resource of Jace's hands, imagination and love, and the trip was so great that I wasn't worried about the destination.

When I was somewhere around Jupiter, Jace murmured something that didn't travel well through space. He stepped away for a second, though he kept reaching out to stroke my spine or lay his hand on my throbbing butt, as if to say *I'm right here.* I squirmed within my yarn cocoon, my yarn rocket, the yarn that extended Jace's arms so he could hug me even when his hands were busy. I heard the sound of a zipper, a rustle of fabric. My cunt clenched in anticipation.

Something smacked my hot, tender ass. It wasn't Jace's hand and it didn't feel like our old friends the crop, the leather slapper or the repurposed ping-pong paddle. It stung and thudded at the same time, hurting in a deep, delicious, cutting way, like a cane—except we didn't have a cane. It was cool and hard. It didn't wrap at all.

I had my suspicions, but unable to push myself up, I couldn't see behind me enough to get a good look.

Before I could make my foggy brain formulate a question or squirm around enough to see what this mysterious new toy was, Jace used it again. I shrieked as a thin line of fire seared into my ass.

While I was still shrieking, Jace brought it into my view: a size 9 aluminum knitting needle, as pink as my ass.

Which he hit again with the awful-slash-wonderful thing.

Jace tugged on the harness, shifting the yarn that ran between my legs just enough to tease my clit. The intense pain trans-muted into equally intense pleasure. I exploded into stars, only the yarn bonds keeping me knit into the fabric of earth and not actually shooting through the roof and into the Milky Way.

While I was still convulsing, Jace shoved aside the yarn at my crotch and entered me. One quick thrust, no subtlety at all, and then, before I had a chance to become accustomed to the sensation, he leaned over me and began to pound. My poor, tender butt felt spanked all over again each time his hips crashed into me, and my bound arms, caught between my body and Jace's, protested. I felt every wrap of the scratchy yarn as if it was three times its actual thickness. My muscles ached.

I loved it.

I was moaning and screaming and begging Jace not to stop, each stroke, each fresh challenge pushing me further. "That's it," Jace snarled. "Come for me, love. Come on my cock." It wasn't like I had much choice at that point. The nasty, tender words tightened the bonds, stroked my clit, and I came again as Jace did, even harder than before.

I was too dazed, too hoarse from crying out, to say anything other than "Wow. Love you," as Jace untied me.

But once I was curled on the bed next to him, staring at a damp, sweaty snarl of yarn, I couldn't resist saying, "I told you yarn was addictive."

"I see what you mean," he agreed. "But that orange stuff still has to go."

EIGHT P.M. APPOINTMENT TEE VEE

Victoria Janssen

Tuesday nights are their television nights. When they meet, Sven hasn't seen Martha's favorite show, on the air for only three episodes. Martha is already in love with the tweedy mentor character, Knightley. She and Sven fuck for the first time after Knightley's big episode, number nine, in which his risqué youth is revealed due to a magic spell and she gets to see Knightley onscreen in a skintight T-shirt.

She and Sven lie in a sticky tangle on her carpet afterward. Martha asks him if he had a risqué youth.

His youth was her childhood. He gives her a significant look. Martha tweaks his nipple. He says, "Does doing it in the back of a pickup count?" He pauses, hand stroking the rounded bit just below her navel. He adds, "It was a parade."

A lot of the time the funny things he says aren't meant to be jokes, his mind just works that way. Martha loves that about him. Also how he looks when she finally gets him unbuttoned from his suits and ties.

She imagines naked Sven humping some Beauty Queen of the Flyover Dairy Cows while the Beauty Queen tosses candy to a screaming crowd. Martha has a bizarre imagination. She pokes him in the stomach.

"After the parade," he explains. "Me and Karen Hazilik. Crepe paper is nasty when it dries on you. Do people even decorate with crepe paper anymore?"

"Let's do it in a pickup," Martha says. "Up at Steamy Point. We'll pretend we're teenagers, making out." This is a test. She wants to know if he's willing to play along with her weirder inspirations.

"We can't take all our clothes off. That'd be cheating." He leers. "I'll be your naughty teacher."

"Let's go Friday. Wear a tight T-shirt."

Their trip to the Point works out really well and soon they are seeing each other several times a week. Sven comes over every Tuesday around seven so they have time for pizza and beer before Martha's show comes on. Sven starts to like it, too, but he likes different characters: the fraternity brothers who are telepathic, but only with each other, because of a ritual and a lightning strike and a family of cheerleader witches. They can see ghostly images of murder.

Martha thinks the college guys are totally doing it, and tells him so while she's getting his boxers off.

"They are not!" Sven chokes out. Then he whimpers when she kisses the end of his cock.

Sven is breathing faster. "Are you…would you want to watch them fuck? Two men? Like men like watching two women."

Martha doesn't have to think about that. "Definitely. They're both hot." She thinks about it a minute, then adds, "They could make a Knightley sandwich."

Sven blushes some more. "You know people write these stories.

On the Internet." He combs his fingers through her hair; it's short and dark and curly, a bit like one of the guys on their show.

Martha is fascinated with what he's just revealed but she's busy right now. She licks around the head of his cock in teasing circles and watches his face change. "We'll Google when we're done," she suggests, and starts sucking his cock in earnest.

Sven's head falls against the back of the couch. "Oh, god, Martha, don't stop."

She pumps his lower shaft with her hand and takes time to lick his balls, enjoying the soft buzz of furry skin against her tongue and the way his belly tightens and twitches. She smooths her free hand over his abs, which aren't cut but are nice and solid.

"Push down," he begs.

He likes it when she strokes and presses around his cock while she's sucking him. She's figured out that shifting the compression of her hand diverts sensation from his cock and helps him to last longer. She loves experimenting with him to make him feel good. He's been trying the same thing when he goes down on her, mostly using the heel of his hand or the ball of his thumb in unexpected places. She thinks of it as "pleasure pinball."

They never get around to Googling that night. On Saturday they find stories where the college buddies are doing it with Samantha, the show's only female character. In one story, they've all been turned into vampires, and in another, they're all writers living in Paris in the 1920s. Sven bookmarks those. Then Martha finds the ones (there are lots) where the guys are doing it with each other, no girl in sight. Also a story where both guys do it with Knightley, which she bookmarks, and another one where Knightley makes them wear neon nylon dog collars and put lipstick on each other using only their mouths and fuck each other with dildoes and a bunch of other kinky things. The blond one cries a lot but it doesn't stop him from having a giant woody the whole time. It turns out Knightley is doing it all because he's pregnant from a magic spell and not allowed to have sex himself for eleven months.

Martha reads the last story aloud while Sven rolls on the carpet, moaning, begging her to stop because it's so awful, a thousand times worse than any student paper he's ever read, even in his introductory classes. It's true the dialogue is terrible, and there's too much repetitive description, but Martha thinks it's hilarious, and every time she puts on Knightley's English accent giving commands, Sven laughs so hard he can't breathe and bangs his head on the floor.

Martha finally takes pity on him and stops. She decides to go back later to see if she can find some better threesome ones where Knightley is not magically pregnant. Then Sven streams some gay porn for her, which Martha thinks is really hot. She picks out which guys in the movie look most like the telepathic guys. Sven eventually gets into it a little bit because she likes it, even though he says all the naked men make him think of locker rooms instead of sex. Also, he can't believe their cocks are really that big. Maybe it's the camera angles.

They make out on and off through the whole thing, and Martha decides tonight is the night she wants to try anal sex together. That needs the bed, so they switch off the porn and find the lube.

It turns out Sven hasn't done anal before. Martha gets a thrill out of that and takes over as teacher. Sven's a little scared and cautious, so they spend a long time on foreplay. Sven massages her from shoulders to feet before he starts working on her ass.

She convinces him to rim her—she's never had anyone do that for her before, so it seems fair as well as unspeakably hot—and he figures out the best techniques on his own, sliding his hand between her legs while he tongues her hole. The sensations are delicate and fluttery and prickly all at once. She forgets everything except how good it feels. After she comes, pulsing hard around Sven's fingers, she murmurs, "Prep time."

Sven points out that the guys in the movie just went right to it. She reaches into a drawer and brandishes one of her dildoes. "You want to try it?"

Sven gets a funny look on his face. "Maybe?"

That's intriguing. Martha squirts lube onto his fingers. "Tonight I want *you* to fuck *me*."

She flinches after he slips a fingertip into her, because she's so sensitive from the rimming. Sven jerks back. "No, no," she says. "It's okay. I'm just twitchy."

He makes her turn over and look at him. "You're sure." He doesn't sound nervous anymore, probably because of the way he just made her come wailing, and Martha gets a little thrill because he's hardly ever like this in bed, in charge, unless they're playing a game like naughty teacher.

"Do it," she says. "I want your cock in my hole."

His eyes get even darker at the way she says it, and he shoves her back onto her stomach. She probably shouldn't be getting him this excited when anal needs patience, but she's eager and this isn't her first time. She's sure she can take him comfortably.

Martha relaxes into his delicate massage as he works in more fingers one at a time, getting her ready for his cock. She breathes deep, relaxing, shivering at how good it feels when he shifts the position of his fingers. Finally, she says she's ready. Actually, she looks over her shoulder and says, "Take me, Knightley!"

Sven swats her ass. He's hard as a rock. "Condom," he demands. Martha grins and puts it on him with her mouth. Then he takes her from behind, not at all tentative, his cock a steady stretch, shoving the breath out of her in a long moan. Sven gets partway inside her and stops, panting. "I still don't believe they're doing it," he says, and thrusts home.

Martha is laughing, which moves his cock inside her in ways that make her shake and clench. "I'll show you evidence next week," she gasps out. "Now fuck me."

Sven doesn't last all that long but neither does she. It's messy and sweaty and feels sensational. Afterward, they cuddle up, sticky as they are, and talk quietly in the weird yellow light of a street lamp outside Martha's window.

Sven says a couple of the other soccer players on his college team were gay; they were together, but always said they weren't a couple. Once in a while they'd tell him how incredible gay sex was and let him know that if he was ever curious, he could stop by their place and get educated. They were kidding, sort of. But if he'd ever stopped by, he thinks they would have done what they said. Sometimes he wonders what would have happened. It would never happen in real life. They finally admitted they were in love, moved to Toronto, and got married. He says, softer than before, that he thinks about them sometimes when he masturbates.

Martha tells him what it was like growing up with her three brothers. She always wished she was a boy, too. She didn't understand girls and why they liked dresses and Disney princesses when she liked Star Wars and lightsaber fights. All her friends at school were boys. When they hit puberty, suddenly all her friends wanted to be her boyfriend. That weirded her out because she thought she was one of them, not one of those girls that sneak off into hallways to let a boy stick his tongue in her mouth. That's when she got curious for the first time about what boys could do together. She went to the bookstore and read a bunch of gay erotica. It was the first time she'd read anything sexy like that.

Sven asks her if she ever imagines she's a man while she's

fantasizing, and she says yes. She tells him one or two scenarios. Then she sits up and rests her hand in the middle of his chest, right over his heart. She tells him that she didn't do that while he was rimming her, or while he was fucking her. Then, she was just Martha and Sven was fucking her. She can be herself with him. That's why she loves him.

Sven tells her, like it's a secret, that he loves her.

The next Tuesday, they cuddle up on the couch under a big comforter. It's fall sweeps on TV, and the temperature outside dropped unexpectedly yesterday. Martha likes fondling Sven's thigh underneath the blanket; it feels dirtier than doing it out in the open like usual. Whenever the college buddies come on screen, she points out to Sven how close they're standing.

"They're standing really close to Samantha, too," he points out.

"They're not looking at her," she says. "Look how Jamie touches Ben all the time."

"They're friends." Sven kisses her neck. "Besides, Knightley's always touching Ben, too."

"Ben is the fuck bunny on this show," Martha says.

Sven starts laughing into her neck. He nips her behind her ear, where she likes it, and she slides her hand higher up on his thigh. He says, "Do you want me as much as you want Knightley?"

"You wouldn't mind, would you?" she says. "If he came over. We could have a threesome. I wouldn't make you touch his dick if you didn't want to." She kisses his cheek, a big smacking one. "You know *you're* my Knightley."

They end up wrestling for possession of Sven's cock under the comforter, and getting all tangled in it, so they almost miss the big scene where Samantha kisses Jamie, and Jamie rejects her.

"Shit!" Martha says. "I was right! He *is* doing Ben! How else could he ignore those knockers?!"

"Let's go to bed," Sven says, in a faint voice, because Martha is still stroking his cock with both hands and he's hard as a rock.

"Let's do it doggie-style, so we can both watch. There's another half hour left."

It's actually really hard to watch TV and have sex at the same time, even if you're enthusiastic. Martha keeps making Sven stop when there's important dialogue and start up again when there's a fight scene. He bitches and groans but he does it because he's watching, too. The starting and stopping turns out to be really hot.

Samantha, it turns out, might be possessed by a demon. Or might not. It's hard to tell. Martha wonders if the demon gave her better cleavage than she'd had in the previous week's episode.

Knightley does spells while Samantha's tied up, and there's a lot of writhing and moaning. Sven asks Martha if *she's* possessed because she makes those moaning noises all the time. He asks if he can tie her up and do some spells. She can't smack him because he's behind her, his cock in her cunt.

A commercial blasts on but Martha can't reach the remote. "Fuck me, fuck me!" she yells, and Sven fucks her so fast her eyes cross. They both come by the time the commercial break is over, which is a good thing, because the scene has shifted and the story is back with Jamie and Ben.

"Pay attention, it's your guys," she says. She takes the condom off him and throws it away, then sits on the back of the couch with her feet on Sven's chest. He's taking up all the room.

Sven groans. "Was that an earthquake?"

On the TV, Jamie and Ben are doing a ritual. Both of them have to contribute blood to the ingredients. Martha pokes Sven with her foot and points out how tenderly they cut each other, which wakes Sven up enough to roll on his side and watch.

"Jamie *licked* him," he says. "I'm not sure if that's hot or not."

"He didn't have to lick that blood," Martha says. "Do you think he got turned into a vampire when he was missing last week?"

The background music is swelling. Ben's crouched over his middle, rocking back and forth. Jamie has his hand on Ben's head, petting his hair, and they're both panting. It's unclear if they're trying to save Samantha from the demon, or destroy the demon and Samantha both, or if this has nothing to do with Samantha at all; they could be seeing a vision of a murder. The one from earlier in the episode, that might have been committed by a possessed Samantha. Is Ben possessed? Regardless, Sven looks at Martha and says, "You were right. They're totally doing it."

There's a big flash on the screen. The scene cuts to Knightley. His eyes are glowing and he has his hands on Samantha, but he keeps repeating Ben's name.

"Uh-oh," Martha says. Knightley shrieks, and the credits roll. Cliffhanger. "Fuck!" Martha yells.

Sven wraps his hand around her ankle and hugs it. "I hope nobody gets killed off."

"They can't kill anyone off yet, it's too early in the season," Martha says. "Jamie and Ben haven't even kissed yet. They have a long way to go."

Sven drags her down on top of him and cuddles her. In a Knightley accent he says, "So do we, love. So do we."

NINE P.M.
VICTORIA
COACH STATION

Kate Pearce

In the dank chill of a London winter's night, Victoria coach station gleamed like a tacky Vegas oasis of neon and desperation. While she froze her ass off, Julia had plenty of time to wonder why they hadn't renamed it. Coaches made her feel all Colin Firth and tight breeches and Gretna Green. One of the reasons she'd come to London was to experience the sense of history, but the dreary transportation hub wasn't exactly what she'd pictured. The sense of anticipation, of sad partings and joyous meetings, however, she guessed remained the same.

She hadn't expected the bone-deep cold that made her California-acclimatized body constantly tremble. And why the hell was she standing out here at nine in the evening, when she could be tucked up in bed with a cup of cocoa, warming her feet on a hot water bottle? She'd taken to those small British comforts immediately.

She checked her cell. The bus was already late, but there weren't any messages. Not that he knew she was waiting for him anyway. With a sigh, she leaned back against the crumbling brick wall and watched as another huge bus, headlights blazing, squeezed its way through the narrow entranceway. The roar of the engine bounced off the surrounding walls. Julia flinched and stuck her gloved hands more firmly into her pockets.

The bus stopped right in front of her, and the doors opened with a gush of warm fetid air to disgorge the passengers. She watched the people descend, and had almost given up hope when she saw him, battered backpack, black leather jacket, blue jeans and cowboy boots. Her breath escaped her in a slow drawn-out wave that condensed in the freezing air. She made no move toward him as other people were doing, no move to welcome him at all, her fingers now buried in the brickwork behind her, her expression, she hoped, showing nothing.

He saw her, his blue gaze penetrating, as he hefted his back-pack and slowly walked toward her. Six foot three, two hundred and fifty pounds of prime American male.

"Hey." He hesitated as she licked her lips. "I didn't expect you to be here."

She shrugged. "Neither did I."

He moved closer until his body shielded her from the lights and the noise of the station. "Then why did you come? You made your choice."

"Did I?" She just stared up at him, her hungry gaze roaming over the lush curve of his lower lip, his dark stubble, his familiar spicy scent.

"Julia…"

She reached up and cupped his cheek. "I…wanted to see you."

He made an exasperated sound and moved his head until his mouth grazed her palm. The sensation of his unshaven chin made her shudder, made her want to press herself against him and never let go. He bit the fleshy mound below her thumb and she moaned.

"Please, Michael."

"I can't give you what you want, Julia. We've been through this."

She slid her gloved hand around the back of his neck and jerked his head down to meet hers, licked his lips in a deliberate invitation, which he took, his tongue in her mouth taking possession of hers. She kissed him back until they were both gasping, and suddenly aware of a little group of gawkers who had gathered around to mock.

"Not here," Michael muttered.

In answer, Julia grabbed for his hand and walked him toward the exit. He was strong enough to reel her back in less than three paces.

"I can't leave here. I have another bus to catch."

"I get that."

She yanked on his hand again, and this time, he let her lead him around the corner of the building to a narrow alleyway, which seemed uninhabited by either dossers or rats. Julia stopped and he was on her, pressing her back against the unforgiving wall, his mouth ravaging hers, his body even through all the layers of clothing a hard, persistent presence she wanted to wrap her legs around and climb.

His hand delved beneath her buttoned-up coat and found the hem of her long woolen skirt, dragged that up and was between her legs rubbing at her panties in a hard, unforgiving rhythm that made her squirm against him.

"Fuck, you're wet," he murmured against her mouth.

Fuck, yes, fuck me, Julia silently pleaded as he unzipped his jeans and shoved them down just enough to release his cock. And god, there he was, big and hard and shoving himself between her legs, impaling her in his hurry to make this as quick and fast as possible. She understood why, she knew what he was trying to tell her but it didn't matter. Just a body, just a fuck. All that mattered was the feel of his flesh inside her making her even wetter, making her come all around him. Even as she climaxed, he kept going, each stroke a brutal invasion that kept her pinned against the wall like an insect speared on a pin.

Julia closed her eyes and held on as his thumb found her already swollen clit and rubbed it in time to his thrusts, sending her to a new plateau of sensations that made her want to cry. Had he always been this big, this rough, or was this what she'd done to him when she'd sent him away?

"Julia..." He whispered her name when he came, the heat of him inside her warming her from the inside out, defrosting the coldness she'd encased herself in ever since he'd left.

He held her close, his forehead resting on her shoulder, her whole body engulfed by the raging heat of his. "What are you going to tell him when you get home?"

Julia wanted to turn her head away but her hair was trapped behind her. "I won't need to tell him anything."

He pushed his hips against hers. "You don't think he'll notice that you've been fucked?" Inside her, his cock jerked and started to fill out again. "You don't think he'll notice my come is dripping out of you and that you smell of me? He knows what we smell like together. He fucking knows." He started rocking against her again, each movement bringing his cock back to life and reigniting the overload of sensations. "Maybe I'd better fuck you again so that he can't miss it, make you so sore that you can't sit down tomorrow. Do you think he'll notice that?"

His mouth claimed hers again, and he fucked her, this time shorter, but definitely not sweeter. She felt every grind of his hips against hers, every pulse of his shaft inside her. When his thumb circled her clit, she tensed.

"Don't, I can't, I'm too sore."

"Too late, Julia, you should've stayed home with him if you wanted someone not to push you."

This time when she climaxed, she screamed into his mouth and he came with her, each spurt of come forced out of him in long, lingering waves. She would be wet tomorrow; even if she showered, she'd still be showing the evidence of his fucking.

He nipped at her ear. "You'll have to go home on the tube now, like this, every man on that train knowing you've been fucked, with my scent and my come all over you."

"Yes," she whispered.

He caught hold of her chin and made her look at him. "You are going home. I'm not taking you with me."

She met his gaze. "I didn't ask you to."

He slowly pulled out of her and zipped up his jeans, one hand steadying her against the wall. "Did you get what you wanted from me, Julia?"

She shook her head, and his expression tightened. "Well, that's a damn shame, because that's all I have to give you."

He turned away and she closed her eyes, unwilling to watch him walk away from her again, unable to watch him at all. It took all her strength not to call out to him, not to beg him to stay, or let her go with him, but she wouldn't do it.

When she finally opened her eyes, he was still there, blocking the exit to the passageway.

"I thought you were going."

"I reckon I have time to buy you a coffee."

She blinked at him. "But you have to go."

He sighed. "I know, but I'm a fucking idiot." He held out his hand. "There's an all-night café on the corner."

She took his hand and followed him to the café. Strip lighting beamed down on greasy Formica-topped tables and the air was heavy with the scent of stale cooking oil. The metal-legged chair shrieked a protest against the tiled floor when she pulled it out. The occupants of the café were mainly teenagers, night-shift workers and people like her who had no idea where else to go.

Michael went up to the counter and ordered something without consulting her, but at this point she didn't care. Her legs were trembling and her body felt as if she'd run a hundred miles. She checked that her gloves were still in her pockets and took off her hat.

"Here you go."

Michael slid a big mug of tea across the table to her.

"That's not coffee."

"Surely you've learned by now not to drink the stuff here? The Brits are right. Tea is the drink for all occasions."

She clasped the mug between her cold hands and inhaled the steam. It didn't matter what beverage she drank, only that it gave her something to do with her hands.

"Where are you off to now?" she asked, not looking at him.

Silence greeted her question. She quickly sipped at her tea, burning her already swollen lip.

"How did you know I was going to be here tonight, Julia?"

She gave him his silence back. Two could play at that game, and wasn't that what this was? A big, stupid game?

"Did he tell you?" Michael cursed under his breath. "He must have done. Why the hell did he tell you? Does he just like to stir the shit, or is it worse than that?"

She glanced up at him and wished she hadn't as he held her gaze, his blue eyes so weary, so weary of her that she wanted to cry.

"Is that what you do now, Julia? Play his fucking games,

do his fucking will?" His harsh laughter bounced off the dirty glass window, but no one looked up. "He must have expected you to come and see me."

"He didn't tell me. I just saw a note on his calendar."

"God, Julia, don't be so naïve. If he wrote it down in public view, he *wanted* you to know."

"I..." She tried to form the words to deny his claims, but they wouldn't come. Michael had always been the one to decipher the lies from the truth for her. Without him, she was lost. But he'd known that, and he'd still left. Left her alone.

She rose to her feet, pushing the chair back with a screech of metal on tile that mirrored the sounds spiraling like a death lament inside her. "I have to go."

He grabbed for her wrist. "*Shit*, Julia, I didn't mean it, don't..."

She shook him off and headed for the door. They'd both used her, they always had. Maybe it was time for her to accept that and either deal with it or run back home to the safety of California.

"Julia." He spun her around by the shoulder. "Listen to me..."

She pressed her cold fingers to his warm lips. "It's okay, I get it now. I thought it was about me, but it isn't really, is it? It's about you and Dan. I'm just your latest chew toy." She took a deep steadying breath. "Do you know what I'm going to do? I'm going to go home and tell him everything we did together. Show him the marks on my body, your sweat, and your come in me."

Michael swallowed hard and she saw the truth in his eyes.

"That's why you did it, wasn't it?" she whispered. "For him? Not for me at all. You *want* him to see you in me, smell you, taste *you*."

His hand dropped to his side, his fist clenched. "It's not that simple, Julia. It never is."

"Sure it is." She looked him right in the eye. "And you know what? I'm okay with that. You go off and find yourself, and I'll keep your best friend happy." She fumbled in her pocket for her cell phone and handed it to him. "But you text me when you come through London again, okay?"

He took the phone, and after a moment's hesitation punched his number in.

"Thank you." Julia slipped the cell into her pocket. "Now you can go."

TEN P.M. PORTRAITS

Preston Avery

She told him he wouldn't regret it. And he didn't, not one bit.

"Eight megapixels, Mal! Do you have any clue what I can do with eight megapixels on a smartphone?" He sure as hell did now.

After a few seconds of fumbling, a flash sparked bright and otherworldly in the dim sitting room, the place where people normally tossed their jackets. It was 10:00 p.m. exactly, and Mal pushed the rest of the way into the hot waiting center between his wife's spread legs. The heaviness of their breath, their shared lust almost visibly charged the air around them in the burst of light. It made Mal think of lightning, and he pounded into her, his beautiful, loving and utterly fuckable Eve. All day he had been building to this, waiting for this. To be hard and hot inside her.

He was so glad he had bought her that damn phone. Mal was unusually non-gadgety for an engineer and had always preferred stars, planets and galaxies to technology, so when Evelyn had asked him for the $600 phone with its multitude of megapixels, he hadn't understood the need. He mainly used his phone for the antiquated practice of calling people, so megapixels didn't mean a lot to him. In the end, though, eight megapixels made Evelyn happy, so Evelyn got eight megapixels. At this exact moment, he was keen on his own generosity, pleased as he licked her neck and tasted salt, glad as she clutched at him with more than hands. He held his thumb to her clit and waited, pushed, prayed for her to break. When she did, he did too, and it was glorious. Somewhere he was sure a star had just collapsed into itself the way he collapsed into her. The entire day had proven to be an education in exactly what Evelyn could do with those eight megapixels. Later they would look at the picture they had made together, artless, probably fuzzy and off center, but spectacularly obscene. They would see just how sweet a sight their joining could be. Right now, though, he kissed her clavicle and thought about the first photograph she had sent him.

It had come at eleven a.m.

Sitting in the conference room, he discreetly slipped his vibrating mobile out of his pocket while feigning interest in the latest stupidity-induced safety incident at the East Plant. It took him a second to realize the photo on his screen was not exactly fit for present company. The curve of his wife's neck from right below her chin to her collarbone, a smooth expanse of creamy white skin, was such an unexpected image and so suddenly intimate his cock stirred. Instantly uncomfortable, he shoved the cell into his pocket, cleared his throat and forced his attention back to idiot contractors and the painful amount of paperwork piled on top of him.

Once alone and in his office, Mal found himself smiling,

fantasizing a little. He realized he had been daydreaming long enough for his desktop computer to hibernate. He pulled up the photo for a more thorough examination. There was no accompanying text, but the vulnerability of her offered throat whispered sweet private things. She was distracting him, but it felt good. He tried to call her so he could tell her, but she didn't answer.

In his department's small kitchenette, he made two open-faced sandwiches and was about to crack his new book *Black Holes and Time Warps: Einstein's Outrageous Legacy* when his phone vibrated a second time. Eve's feet were displayed prettily, positioned on a pillow from their bed. She had painted her toenails red. Not red, but *red* red. He had a real thing for *red* red. Redial. Voice mail. A few moments later, she sent him the same image but in black and white.

The time was 12:02 p.m.

At one o'clock, she sent an image of her mouth. Glossy. *Red* red. She was biting her bottom lip.

At two, the inside of her right elbow where she had a tiny heart tattooed.

At three, her belly button.

The four o'clock picture took some deciphering, but when he finally realized where her hand rested with its short red nails, the twitch he had come to expect became more insistent. The inside of her thigh. He had a thing for the inside of her thigh too. Just like her feet and belly button, her mouth, elbow and *red* red. He scrolled through the other images and suffered a brief moment of insanity when he considered rubbing one out in the bathroom. He wasn't used to being so preoccupied at work, but he did like where she was taking him.

Mal's boss walked into his office at three minutes to five. "I need you to stick around."

Of course he did.

"Some insulated pipe coming out of the second catalytic reactor at the SRU is smoking."

Of course it was.

"You're gonna have to coordinate the emergency response team with the in-unit personnel in case they can't mitigate it."

When Eve's five p.m. photo came, he took a second to admire the close-up shot of her cleavage and even less imagining his face there. The SRU wasn't the only unit on fire today. He texted to say he would be late for her father's birthday dinner, that he would probably just have to meet them there. What he got in return was a picture of her lips in an exaggerated pout. Even through these years together and everything that came with them, she could still make him laugh, and he still wanted her. So much.

Six o'clock came, and Mal was so intent on his H2S monitor that his phone's buzz startled him. The human body is flexuous, with bends and dips and curves. It has seams too—places where skeletons might have been snapped together if bodies were made in factories, if skin and muscle, joints and bone were assembled robotically. What Eve showed him now was far less mundane than a joint or a hinge, though. That inside place where her leg met torso, that slight little dip displaying on one side a span of thigh, and on the other, secret, mounded flesh seemed a hallowed place. He was compelled to touch the screen even though that felt foolish.

An hour later when Mal pulled into the parking lot of Luciano Ristorante, his cell went off again. Alabaster roundness crowned with light brown areola, and tight, darker, crinkled nipple. He glanced to where Eve was handing her keys to the valet. There must be some type of text scheduler on her phone. While he had been kept on pins and needles all day, slowly tortured hour by hour, his dearest had probably taken the pictures in a matter of minutes. He thought about her taking them, turning herself on as she made plans and painted her nails. *Flash.* Twisting her nipple. *Flash.* Thrusting three fingers into that pink place where she would be saturated, thinking of him. *Flash.* Getting off before she had sent her first picture. *Flash.*

From here, she seemed to be throwing something off, energy, hot like the sun or a pulsar. Mal realized that somewhere along the way he had forgotten she could shine with such fundamental sexuality, glow with desire. He stared at her. His wife.

By the time eight o'clock came around and Mal had looked at the photo, they had devoured wine, apps and salad. They had also balanced the national budget. He swallowed a sound but Eve refused to look at him. Her nipple was still the focal point but framed within a red-nailed thumb and forefinger. Pinching. Twisting. Killing him.

"Work?" his father-in-law asked. "They've sure had you up against a wall today." Mal concurred, all the while refusing to picture the man's only daughter up against a wall. Well, mostly refusing.

Mal's gaze constantly strayed to her, his mind too. It had been a while since they had taken time for more than a quickie in the missionary position. Ironically, though, he was so ready to go right now, he wasn't sure he could last much longer than that anyway. He felt like he was falling in new love, the enormity of his entire world, the whole galaxy orbiting a single point, single person. Eve. She was eating dessert, wrapping her mouth around the spoon, licking the traces of chocolate from her lips. Buzz. Fortunately Jack and Madeline were asking the server about post-dinner port. Mal had barely survived dessert. He leaned over to her. "Never knew I had such restraint." He quickly bit her earlobe and noticed pink creep up her neck. He thumbed on his phone as Eve excused herself.

"Jesus," he breathed, then watched her walk away, but all he actually saw was a high-contrast image of her wide-spread legs with a finger pressing her little clit nice and tight. That finger might as well have been a flashing neon arrow to her slit: *Enter here, open all night.* Then she sent him an actual text message: *I'm in no mood for Port.* He had to bite back a hallelujah.

They drove home separately. It made him crazy. Each image flashed through his mind now, a seductive flipbook that stirred anticipation inside him to such a degree he swore he might go supernova. It felt good to be so close to snapping, though, to losing it, to showing her all the skill and stamina of a fourteen-year-old with his first *Playboy.* He vowed against that, though. He would make this good for her. That would be his gift just as the pictures had been hers.

She beat him to the house but waited outside the front door. She had found the time to reapply her lipstick. He pushed her against the doorbell, not meaning to set it off, but ignored the incessant dinging as he shoved his tongue into her mouth and ran rough, urgent hands over as much of her as he could get at. He was pressing his hips into hers, loving the pressure, the building moans in her throat, the wildness.

When she broke away, they were both giddy and breathless. He unlocked and opened the door.

"I want it all off, Evelyn. And you on the couch." He pointed toward the sitting room. She nodded and reached down to pull the flowered T-shirt over her head, stepping slowly backward. Mal watched, mirroring her actions—shirt, pants, then underwear. There wasn't much light, just a few lamps left on, but it was perfect illumination, dusky and warm, like all the edges of life were blurred. By the time they were completely naked, the backs of her knees had met the smooth velour sofa. That couch had been their first major purchase as a couple and had seen a lot of action. It was about to see some more. They stood apart, two partners, two lovers, separated and wanting, but neither moved closer. Mal reached down and deliberately fisted his dick. His own touch felt gratifying, especially as Eve's eyes followed the motion of his hand and her white teeth dug into that *red* red bottom lip.

"I thought I told you to get on the couch." Eve snapped out of her voyeuristic fog and sat down. "Lean all the way back, arms out by your sides." She obeyed him. "Spread your legs for me, baby." And she did that too, though after a brief hesitation.

He walked toward her, not letting his rhythm falter. The tug was serving to bring his boil down. If he could reach more of a simmer, it would keep him from tearing her apart. He could smell her, and standing between her open knees, he reached down with his free hand to feel her.

"Do you remember the first time, Eve?"

"The bonfire."

"I had to eat dinner with your parents that night too."

She smiled. "We were so young. Just kids, really."

"The way I felt that night, when I finally talked you out of your skirt and those little panties with the bows. I swear to god that's how I am going to feel tonight. When I push into you. When I split that gorgeous little slit of yours."

She flushed at his words. Mal couldn't see in the near dark, but he knew it, just like he knew how much she liked it when he talked to her this way.

He released himself, and she licked her lips, watching that very male part of him bob against his belly. He was enamored by the way she did that. Looked at him there. "Let's reflect on our day, shall we, Eve?" Her wide eyes flicked to his face. "Eleven a.m.," he said, then bit the curve of her neck. He felt goose bumps break out on her skin and licked the spot.

"Noon," he told her, then knelt down to the carpet, raising her left foot to kiss each toe, then her right. "12:02." He repeated the attentions to her feet.

"One p.m." He stood up and leaned over her, placing his hands on the couch, flanking her head. He kissed her mouth, slowly at first, but building until she parted her lips for him. He thrust his tongue inside twice. He bit her lip as he pulled away. She cried out. They were both reeling.

"Two." Mal licked the tattoo at the inside of her right elbow.

"Three." His mouth briefly skimmed her belly button.

"Four." He was becoming impatient and breathed the word into her inner thigh before moving to "Five." He squeezed her breasts together, making sure to tweak her nipples, then paused for dramatic effect before soundly motorboating her. They both laughed, full-body, racking laughter. That felt so good too. He said, "5:12," and barely touched his smiling lips to hers.

"Six." He slowly began tracing the seam where her leg met her torso, delicate, pale, private skin being caressed by rough, callused fingertips.

"Seven." He took her left nipple into his mouth, the steady sweeping movement of his fingers unrelenting, just the same as the stroke on his own cock before. He felt her gasp and shiver beneath his touch, his tongue. Sucking and licking and biting. He pulled back, stretching her nipple as he held it between his teeth. She cried out in pain, pleasure, impatience. She wiggled, grabbing his head with both hands, tunneling her fingers through his hair, pressing his face, his mouth closer. Another time he might have made sure she put her hands back on the couch. Not now, though. Not tonight. It felt absolute to know how much she needed him.

"Eight. It seems we need to keep those hands busy. Pinch

your nipples." She did, and her eyes were starry, so glazed and fuck-drunk. "You want nine, don't you, baby?" She nodded, but he shook his head. "Say it, and don't you dare let up on those pretty, pretty tits."

"I want it. I want nine." He stared at her, and she stammered, "N-n-nine o'clock. Oh god, Mal, please put your mouth on me." His gaze remained steady, but he cocked his head slightly, so she nearly shouted at him, "My clit, my vagina, my pussy, Jesus God, Mal, please put your mouth on me!"

He did, and she jerked, jolted at the swift contact. "Where's your phone?" he asked into her warm, slick folds. She didn't respond until he repeated the question, licking her in long, slow strokes between each word.

She answered him, but incoherently and in between soft, wet sex sounds. He circled her clit and tapped it twice with the tip of his tongue, then put his fingers there, playing, parting, exploring. He licked a trail up her body to her mouth.

"Eve, reach over to your purse. Get your phone," he said. She did, but with difficulty. When she finally had the $600 wonder in her hands, her arms went limp beside her. "Good. Now. I am going to put my mouth back on your warm"—he kissed her mouth—"starving"—he kissed her again—"wet little cunt, but you will not come." He kissed her longer this time. "Do you understand?"

"Yes," she told him, drawing out the *s* and lolling her head back onto the couch, eyes closed. He stroked indolently inside her and felt her inner muscles clutch at him. He had to keep his pace easy, quiet. That was the only way to keep a rein on himself, keep him from breaking the sound barrier...or something. "Open your eyes, Eve. I want you to pull up your camera." She furrowed her eyebrows in confusion or maybe concentration. He couldn't tell which, but she was doing as he asked, so he slid back down her body to taste her again.

"I have it," she told him.

"Be ready to use it when I say."

She nodded, and he jerked her hips to the edge of the couch, positioning his penis at her entrance. The swiftness of his movement seemed to shock her a little, and she stared wide-eyed, open like the universe. His member seemed to strain toward her like it had a mind of its own.

"Oh god, yes," she said as he gently parted her folds with the point of his prick. Wanting to shove and thrust but gritting his teeth and inching forward instead, he seated himself fully, then pulled out in the same controlled, measured increments. Her hips were pumping off the couch in a gorgeous, graceless rhythm, so he had to hold her more firmly down. She took him so far beyond anything, everything, vast like space itself.

He checked the clock on the wall. It was time. "Now, baby, now." Ten p.m. "Take the picture, Eve. Take it now." And she did.

ELEVEN P.M.
STRIP POKER

Ashley Lister

Strip Poker. The words tightened a knot in Amanda's belly. Surreptitiously, she glanced at Frank. It was eleven o'clock and she didn't know if her excitement came from fear or euphoria or a combination of both. She only knew that as soon as Carl suggested the game, the air in the room was charged with electricity.

Becky sneered. "Do you ever think about anything except sex?"

Carl shook his head. "No. Are you playing?"

There were six of them in the lounge: the last members of a college reunion party that had started four hours earlier at seven o'clock. The table was littered with empty wine bottles and the memories of a pleasant but otherwise unexceptional get-together. Now only the six friends remained.

Carl leant back in his chair and held up a deck of cards. He glanced expectantly at each of them. "Who's in?"

"I'm game." Debbie's enthusiasm didn't surprise anyone.

She pulled up a chair next to Carl.

"Deal me in." Eddie took the seat facing Debbie.

Amanda watched Frank take a chair. She sat down at the table at the same time as him. She could see they were both trying to feign the same air of nonchalance. They had both assumed the studied pose of a person saying, "What the hell! It's only strip poker." As though they played the game every night of the week.

"Becky?" Carl prompted. "Are you playing?"

She rolled her eyes with disdain. "You're never going to grow up, Carl. Are you?" Despite the contempt in her voice, she squeezed between Frank and Eddie.

Amanda tried to quell her excitement. The table was small. They were all sitting so close her knees touched the men on either side. She wondered what that closeness would feel like when they were all wearing less clothing. The idea made her shiver. Her nipples hardened inside her bra. The knot in her stomach tightened.

"Strip poker." Frank grinned. "I can't remember the last time I played."

"It was probably back in college," Eddie chimed in. "Maybe the night of our graduation..."

The anecdotes began as Carl dealt. They exchanged tales of games they had previously played, each more outlandish than the last. Carl's story centered on a girl who had to sit on the laps of all the male players. In Debbie's story the loser was a guy who got rudely fondled by each of the female players. Becky talked about a lone woman who lost to five hung and horny members of the college football team. The salacious tales, each bolder than its predecessor, fueled a fluid longing in Amanda's loins.

She cast a sly glance in Frank's direction.

Their eyes met.

Hurriedly, they each looked away.

Debbie lost the first hand. She shrugged as though the matter meant nothing and peeled off the skintight T-shirt that had been hugging her lithe torso. She wore no bra. Her breasts were bare and her nipples were stiff and dark. The room changed instantly. The air was suddenly too heavy to breathe.

Eddie and Frank whistled. Becky made a disparaging comment about Debbie's lack of a bra. And Carl dealt again.

Carl lost his shirt. Frank was soon down to his boxers. Becky sat in a matching set of expensive lingerie. Eddie remained fully clothed whilst Debbie was down to a thong that hid nothing. Amanda felt self-conscious in her bra and pants. Frank kept glancing at her. His gaze made her squeeze her thighs together, sparking a frisson of delicious sensations.

"What's the loser going to forfeit?" Carl asked.

They all studied him in silence. The anecdotes about previous forfeits had made for heady listening. Amanda swallowed thickly when she realized she could soon become the loser.

"The loser has to kiss a person of the winner's choosing," Eddie suggested.

Carl shrugged. Frank nodded agreement. Debbie started to say that she liked Carl's idea, but Becky interrupted with a suggestion of her own.

Amanda had stopped listening. She thought: *I hope I lose and I have to kiss Frank.* The prospect sent a shiver coursing through her sex. The inner muscles of her pussy clenched with a slow, languorous need. A kiss sounded like a simple enough forfeit, but if she was naked and kissing Frank, she knew the experience would be sensational.

She put down a pair of twos. A losing hand.

Everyone clapped encouragement as she stood up to take off her bra. Exposing her breasts in front of her friends was an odd mixture of liberation and raw, sexual excitement. Eddie, Debbie and Carl all grinned with approval. Frank graced her with embarrassed glances. He shifted uncomfortably in his seat. Her cheeks colored bright crimson as she sat back down wearing only a pair of frilly tangas.

"This could be the last hand," Carl announced. "Are we all okay going with Becky's idea for the forfeit?"

Amanda nodded, even though she couldn't recall what Becky had said. And, when she lost, her head pounded with the dizzying adrenaline rush of stepping out of her panties to expose herself naked to her friends.

Carl and Eddie wolf-whistled. Debbie and Becky clapped with approval.

Frank beamed. "You look ready to make the forfeit."

"What is the forfeit?"

Becky rolled her eyes. "You weren't listening?"

"I must have missed it. What was it?"

Carl laughed and clapped Frank good-naturedly on the shoulder. "Enjoy your prize."

Debbie retrieved her clothes. Eddie stood up and bade everyone a soft-spoken good night whilst Carl helped Becky to dress. Frank was the only one who remained in his seat. He was nearly naked.

"Isn't someone going to tell me what the forfeit is?"

"That's why we're leaving," Carl said. "We figured you and Frank would like some time alone to enjoy that."

Amanda said nothing. Dwelling on the fluid warmth that rushed through her loins, she figured whatever she had to do for Frank, it would be a forfeit she wouldn't mind suffering. Standing coolly to say good night to her friends, no longer troubled by the fact that she was naked, she casually kissed each one good night and wished them a safe journey home. And when they were finally alone, she turned to Frank.

"What forfeit are you expecting?"

He smiled. "You'll like this."

MIDNIGHT: MOVIE DATE

N.T. Morley

M arie drew not stares but glances as she entered the porn
shop.

Even so, she detected the shamed heat of lust radiating from
the men who furtively sized up her lithe form in the tall, tight
trench coat—tall because she was wearing high heels; tight
because she had it buttoned to her throat and belted snugly at
her waist.

About a dozen guys browsed the stacks—a pretty thin crowd
for a shop this big. They tried to ignore her as she browsed. Marie
tried not to rubberneck at the dark, dank corridor at the back of
the shop—the one with the giant sign on one side that said No
Unaccompanied WOMEN In The Preview Section EVER,
and the one on the other side that said YOU Must Buy $5 In
Tokens EVERY Time YOU Enter the Preview Section! She
tried not to look, but she could barely take her eyes off it. To
distract herself while she waited, she cruised easily among the
men, who tried not to look at her and peered uncomfortably

into giant wooden bins filled with shrink-wrapped dongs.

She wandered between racks of cheap, stinky sex toys and wire-frame shelves packed with DVDs under signs that said things like ANAL, GIRL-GIRL, DOUBLE PENETRATION. *They've got a double penetration section?* Marie found herself thinking. *Why can't every business be so lucky?* She couldn't stop glancing back at the "preview section," parts of her going slick that really had no business going slick just yet. But it wasn't her moistening pussy that really bugged her, it was the feeling of energy that coursed through her body. She'd expected to be scared; she really wasn't. She felt like she had these guys by the balls; they seemed far more afraid of her than she did of them. The chance of her getting groped or something—which had seemed so real just moments before she entered the store—now seemed ludicrous at best. Perhaps more importantly, any minute, Aidan was going to walk through that front door. Any errant hand that made its way to her posterior would not be a happy hand if Aidan saw it doing so.

He *would* show up, wouldn't he? *Of course he will,* she told herself. *Didn't that son of a bitch talk me into this?*

She thought about it; she honestly couldn't remember. She figured they'd talked each other into it; that was good enough for her.

As far as she could tell, no one was really using the preview booths. Maybe it was the exorbitant price—$5 in tokens? She remembered the first porn shop she'd ever been to, it was like $1 or something. Or maybe it was just a slow night—after all, it was a Tuesday, about to be a Wednesday. She looked at the clerk, a twenty-something retro kid with chopped-up Sting hair wearing a SILENCE=DEATH T-shirt and paging through an *Entertainment Weekly.* She felt sympathy for the poor bastard; working the graveyard shift at the 24/7 porn shop must get tedious when you were twenty-three or something and queer. Well, she figured, she and Aidan were about to do their part to make the kid's life slightly more interesting. Only slightly, but hey, it was something.

Cruising the sex toy section, Marie spotted something she didn't expect—one of the smoothie-style vibrators came with batteries already installed, a fact proclaimed on the package in hot pink type with multiple exclamation points. *Why the hell didn't I think to bring one?* she thought, and snatched the vibrator up. She felt simultaneously disgusted that sex toy industry copywriters were so lame they'd get that excited about the batteries already being in the damn thing, and excited because now she had a vibrator that was ready to go. Why *hadn't* she thought to bring one, after all?

Well, now she had one—and none too soon. The ancient wall clock over the bored clerk's bleach-blond shrub clicked down to exactly midnight just as Aidan walked through the blacked-out glass door.

Damn, he looked good. Six feet of man in leather pants and engineer boots. Shoulders broader than usual—which was saying something—because he wore his padded jacket. He'd locked his helmet to the bike, so his big, spanky hands were free-range. Marie quivered a little as she wondered whether people ever got spanked at glory holes. *One step at a time*, she told herself. *Blow job*. It made her sweating knees feel weak and her moistening pussy feel tight. She licked her lips and felt the sticky-smooth slime of her bright red lipstick. *Damn, I always do that*, she thought. She wasn't used to wearing lipstick—or for that matter, makeup of any kind. She wasn't especially good at it. Fixing it seemed kind of silly at this point—not to mention *obvious*.

Especially because Aidan had already sized her up with his

big brown eyes—as if he didn't know her, *yum*—and ambled to the counter.

She heard his deep, rich voice intone the magic words:

"Twenty dollars in tokens."

The clerk changed Aidan's bill and counted out twenty $1 tokens. Aidan shot another look at Marie—a *wicked* look, up and down, the bastard. She felt so objectified! It made her nipples hard. How was it the big dumb lug was so unbelievably good at that?

She walked toward the counter, her high heels click-clacking on the cheap linoleum floor. As she passed the preview area, she couldn't resist peering down the hallway. Aidan hadn't gone in yet; he was making a show of reading the movie listings mounted on the wall next to the booth at the end of the hall. But she saw, to her amazement, that the booths that *were* occupied—maybe three out of the twelve or so booths—had little red lights blazing just above the doors. *Holy shit,* she realized, groping after an ancient memory. *Confession. They're just like confessionals.*

Well...maybe not *just* like confessionals. But the confessionals at her church growing up had those same kind of lights above the doors, too, to let you know when they were occupied. God forbid you'd try to scoot in on some *other* schoolgirl uttering her made-up confession. How many times had she knelt in booths just like this at St. Isadora's, a rosary in her hand, her mouth doing something very different than what she was about to do?

Holy shit, was it possible the very same factory made the very same lights for both churches and porn booths?

Marie's brain practically short-circuited at the thought.

Marie stalked to the counter. She forked over her vibrator and a twenty.

"Hi," said the queer clerk cheerfully. "Having a pleasant evening?"

"*Very* pleasant," she said, while he rang up the vibe.

He smiled at her like her status as a woman visiting a porn shop and his status as a queer man working in a porn shop somehow put them on an equal footing, like pervy sisters. She kind of liked that. So after he asked her if she needed a bag and she said no and slipped the vibe into her coat pocket, she probably only need to fork over one Jackson, instead of two. But better safe than sorry.

"Twenty dollars in tokens," she said.

"You've got forty here," the clerk said.

"I think one of those is yours," said Marie.

She smiled.

The clerk gave her a look as if to say, *I would have let you go back there anyway*, but he didn't turn down the bribe. He pocketed one Jackson and put the other in the drawer and counted twenty tokens into Marie's hot little hand.

"Thank you," Marie said, and winked at him.

She'd never been good at winking, so she felt a sense of accomplishment having done it. Did the kid think she was a prostitute? No, she decided. Prostitutes in this neighborhood probably didn't have $20 to pass around. He probably knew what she was—a suburban lady walking on the wild side.

She click-clacked into the corridor between the No Unaccompanied WOMEN sign and the YOU Must Buy $5 In Tokens sign. Aidan saw her coming. He gave her the toothy grin of a man who knows he's about to get a blow job. He ducked into the preview booth. She took the one next to him.

At least he hadn't held the door for her.

* * *

The booth was cramped and tight. It smelled of sex, sweat and bleach. There was a glory hole beneath the video screen—cut or kicked in the wall and lined haphazardly with ancient strips of duct tape.

How many dicks had slid through that hole?

Add one to that number, she thought, imagining Aidan's cock, familiar in their bed—yet unfamiliar, a stranger's, here in a porn booth with a wall between them.

She could hear tokens clinking down the slot in Aidan's booth next door. She heard moans and bad techno as his cinematic experience began just inches away. She fished the tokens out of her coat pocket in handfuls, pumping them in. Her own flick started—a hairy-assed septuagenarian severely rogering a wispy blonde he never could have banged if he hadn't paid her $300. (Actually, no, they were doing anal. Make that $375 or something, Marie decided.) She flipped through the channels and quickly settled on a tall ice-blond dominatrix in a tight latex dress smoking a cigarette in a long holder while a very cute and very nude brunette worshipped the mistress's shiny knee-high boots.

Yum. That would do rather nicely, thanks.

Marie had stuffed a penlight into her pocket—the one she'd just emptied of tokens. She took out the light and scouted for errant pools on the chair and the floor. She didn't find any; it was actually surprisingly clean. The smell seemed to emanate from the trash can, a little pint-sized number that resided just under the wall-mounted tissue dispenser. The former was three-quarters full of half-stiffened used tissues. The latter had a single errant tissue hanging out, wafting in some unfelt breeze like a jellyfish on the tide.

She hit the light again and checked the chair one more time, just to make sure she hadn't missed some prior resident's leavings.

The chair looked fine, but she still wasn't planning to sit there.

It was for her coat, which she shucked quickly, leaving Marie naked—unless you counted her stockings, high heels and knee pads.

The stockings and heels were de rigueur, she felt. How could you give head naked in a glory hole and *not* wear sheer, white, scam-backed lace top stay-ups and sexy white high heels? Unless, of course, you wore black fishnets, but she wasn't *that* kind of slut. She had, after all, once knelt in a booth not much larger than this and worried an antique rosary through her fingers as she made up some bullshit about taking the Lord's name in vain. She was glad she'd never had anything like this to confess in the old days; Old Father Sullivan would have had a heart attack.

The knee pads were a different story. She wouldn't even have thought about doing such a thing if Aidan hadn't suggested it. They were eminently practical; there would be no jizz on her knees, even if she'd missed some. More importantly, at her age she couldn't go fucking around with the health of her knees. She was practically thirty; she had to watch that shit. What more humiliating reason could there be for needing knee surgery at thirty-five? *It's true, Doc. I wore my knees out sucking cock in glory holes.* She much preferred the immediate humiliation of wearing knee pads, which just had something *so dirty* about them. Knee pads. Who wore knee pads? Athletes. She was an athlete, in a sense.

Marie glanced up at the screen and saw the cute brunette leaving red-mouthed kisses all the way up the dominant's long, slender leg. *Double yum.* Before the red mouth could make it to

Candyland, the blond dominatrix grabbed the smaller woman's hair and shoved her face between her thighs.

Marie was just about ready to decide she was a lesbian when Aidan stuck his dick in her face.

She hadn't exactly planned this part, but then again, in any other context she never had any trouble just letting her instincts take over. Marie was a big fan of head; she liked giving it and getting it, but giving it was her selfless pleasure. She did it so damned well that she felt a warm glow of pride whenever she saw a guy she thought was cute, because she knew she could rock his world. Which maybe made it slightly less "selfless" than she pretended, but Aidan didn't seem to mind.

She took his cock in her mouth, feeling the familiar curve, the intimate texture. She went down about halfway, caressing his balls and teasing the lower part of his shaft. She opened wide and aimed her head just right and swallowed him easily— three times in a row, nice and easy, almost effortless. She heard Aidan cursing in amazement, "Jesus, Jesus, fucking Jesus," his obscene and blasphemous moans mingling with those of whatever chippie was caterwauling copiously in rhythmic fakeness from Aidan's chosen porn movie—probably some kind of ass-fuck garbage. But when Marie came up for air, she saw that it wasn't Aidan's porn princess who was yelling like that; it was Marie's own yummy blond dominatrix, making languid O faces while riding the brunette's face. Ugh, Marie hated those fake sounds porn stars made. Tall, Blond and Dominant wasn't so hot anymore. Marie decided maybe she wasn't a lesbian after all, and then she opened wide and took Aidan's cock deep into her throat again.

He moaned, "Jesus, fuck, oh, fuck, oh, Jesus, fuck fuck fuck!" How was it he always seemed so surprised? She really *could* rock his world. Marie felt a warm glow of self-satisfaction...which was when she remembered she had a vibrator just inches away—already loaded up with fresh batteries.

She had to grope a bit, behind her, because she was so unwilling to pause what she was doing. She was enjoying it too much. Having gotten the deep-throating out of the way, she felt she'd impressed Aidan as much as she needed to. Now she could just rock his world with her tongue and her lips and her smooth, soft face, which she rubbed all over his shaft while she lapped at the underside and groped for the vibe in her trench coat pocket.

She found it, got it out and twisted it quickly.

The buzzing started in her hand—hot, heavy and quick.

Twelve bucks and more powerful than the spin cycle.

She settled the vibrator between her legs, letting the tip nestle against her clit for a minute. Pleasure throbbed into her body. She nudged the vibrator down into her slit, teasing her lips apart and feeling how wet she was; after just a minute, the whole vibe felt so slippery she was afraid she might drop it. Without even thinking, she pushed her thighs together, which accomplished two things. It sent an explosive wave of pleasure into her—almost *too* explosive!—and it allowed her to pluck a tissue from the wall-mounted box. She used it to grip the vibe, scandalized and pleased with herself that this whole sleazy scene had gotten her wet enough to make the vibrator almost slip out of her hands. Wow. She really was a slut, wasn't she?

She smelled the mixed-up scents all around her, familiar and alien. Aidan's cock. Her spit. The sticky vinyl scent of the duct tape that lined the glory hole. Aidan's leather pants. His sweat. Other men's sweat, lingering thick on the air-conditioned breeze. The bleach that suffused the booth—hell, the whole *store*. Aidan's precome, musky in her nostrils as she rubbed her face on his cockhead. Other men's scent, wafting up gross from the garbage can. How could a girl as classy as she was think the smell was kinda hot? Weird...it was weird. *She* was weird. She didn't give a fuck.

Pleasure hummed through her. After that, Aidan no longer got the benefit of having two eager hands on his cock; he only got one, but that was more than enough. Marie deep-throated once, just to remind him she could do it, and got the pleasant strains of obscene language as a reward. That made her work the vibrator harder against her clit. She jostled it rhythmically. She was close.

Aidan was closer. Marie had been so lost in the pleasure of servicing him that she hadn't even noticed how close he was getting. When he erupted in her mouth, she had to gulp fast, and she didn't get it all. Aidan's come ran down her chin and onto her tits. She squealed and pushed the vibrator hard against her clit. She felt the come dripping—no, pouring—down her belly, drizzling over her hand as she worked the vibe. Just like always—in their bed, on the couch, a motel room, a dungeon— it was the warm salty flood of Aidan's spend that pushed her over the edge. It wasn't that she was some kind of a freak; she simply needed to know that she'd rocked his world.

She took her mouth off his cock, still drooling everywhere. She looked up at her new girlfriend, the O-face dominatrix; she was still putting on a pretty fake act. Marie put on a much better one, moaning at the top of her lungs as she came. She didn't care who heard—not the queer boy clerk, not the customers. Besides, that dumb dominatrix was doing such a midnight-movie acting job, anyone who heard her would think she was part of the act.

She came hard. She swayed and clutched Aidan's cock for support. She was glad she wore knee pads.

Marie gave herself a minute, leaning her forehead on the side of the glory hole and giving Aidan's cock one last kiss before he pulled it away, stuffed it in his leather pants, and zipped up.

Her flesh goose-bumped. She was getting chilly.

She plucked six more tissues from the box and wiped her face and tits and belly.

She stuffed the soaked tissues through the garbage hole to join their many stinky brothers. Marie gave her howling dominatrix one last disdainful look as she donned and buttoned her trench coat. She tied the belt and stuffed the vibrator into the pocket—this one was a keeper.

As she made for the door, Marie looked the clerk in the eye and smiled at him.

He smiled back.

She tried to wink, but a stray blast of Aidan's come had dried on her temple; it distracted her at a crucial moment.

Oh well. Marie was pretty sure the kid got the idea.

ONE A.M. GIRLS' NIGHT OUT

Vida Bailey

I swing around, pint glass in hand, and there he is. Rob. He's dancing with some girl, and the eye contact he's making looks convincing from her vantage point, but most of the time he's scanning the crowd under the cover of the strobe lights. I try to pretend I don't know he's catching my eye.

Last time I saw him, he was tiptoeing out of my apartment in his socks, collecting his scattered belongings and sneaking out the door. That's why I decided. No more flirty eyes across the bar at kicking-out time, no more grinding on the dance floor. No more shot-for-shot games sitting either side of a bottle on the floor. No more rum- and sweat-soaked orgasms in the small hours, followed by a two-day hangover and a three-day come-down where I cursed my luck with men and whatever perky-breasted bitchslut he was surely sniffing after now.

Nope. Not good for the mental health. I grasped my resolve in my silver-ringed fist and set my sights on surer things.

Tonight, though, those surer things weren't exactly lighting

up my crosshairs. If I'm honest, I've been the one tiptoeing barefoot away from yet another snoring disappointment the last
few Saturday mornings. Those lackluster encounters haven't
been as good for the psyche as I'd anticipated.

So I'd been planning to just go dance with my girls. Thick-
soled, lace-up boots with leggings and a clinging cotton shift
dress. I'm grunging tonight, though the dress does have a
low back. It's one of those nights I feel blessed with my perky
little boobs that push against the cotton without any need for
support. I've got boots and skin and a necklace hanging the
wrong way—my jet beads tight at my throat and hanging down
my spine, pointing like an arrow toward my ass. I tip my head
back and hold my arms out, slopping beer through my fingertips caging the rim of my pint glass, balancing myself with its
weight. No cocktails tonight, no handbags, just lovely, dirty,
sweaty, nostalgic music in the humid, beer-tainted air.

It's dark, but he sees me. I can feel his eyes on me. But I'm
not going to look. He can flaunt all the floozies he likes, I'm
gonna get my dance on and walk home alone.

1:00 a.m. and I'm sitting on the wall outside his flat. Lights on.
I'm a stalker, sitting here, waiting for two silhouettes to cross
the window. It's cold and my ass is going numb on this wall.
I'm fighting the Shoulds pouring through my brain—shouldn't
have severed contact with him, no, should never have slept with
him in the first place, should really be home in bed. I stand up
and look at the window one more time. As I move to leave, my
phone beeps. I don't recognize the number at first because I so
virtuously deleted him from my address book.

*Were you planning to come in, or are you just going to sit
there all night?*

I look up. The window still seems empty. I text back,

desperate for a one-liner that will somehow excuse my undig-
nified behavior.

Do you want me to?

Facepalm. Not so suave. A second ticks by, and his door
swings open, his familiar shape backlit. I jog across the street
and then drag my heels up to his door. He reaches out and runs
a finger up the zip of my scruffy black parka.

"This is nice," he says. "Retro." I smile. I know from his
record collection that we shared similar tastes in the past.

"I'm in fancy dress." He raises an eyebrow, fingers still
lingering on the black canvas. "It's nice to have a warm coat
for the walk home."

"Or for stalking?"

"I wasn't stalking!" Lying indignantly is the best defense.

"Tea?"

So tea will be the stream we float on, until we arrive at a
place that's comfortable again. I sit on the sofa, knees pulled
up, hands clasping a hot mug, and breathe in the steam. I
glance at him while taking a sip. He's looking at me, openly,
and he looks amused. I can feel myself blushing—this is far
harder without the blanket of drunkenness we usually operate
under. I'm not sure what he's waiting for and I look around
the room to buy some time. I've only been here once before,
late at night. The next morning was a sort of stagger-round-in-
sunglasses affair; I didn't remember much about the decor. But
it's nice. Not what I expected. I thought it would be flat-pack
furniture and student squalor, to be honest. But it's a lot more
tasteful than that. Rich neutral colors and reclaimed boards.
Art on the walls. The place must be his, and he's done some
work on it.

"Your place is lovely, Rob." I gesture at the heavy wooden
coffee table and bookcase. He nods at me in acknowledgment.

He cocks his head to one side and studies me and I squirm under his gaze a little.

"Thanks."

There's no "Do you want a tour?" or suggestions about the bedroom. He just keeps watching. "I like your place, too." I frown at my tea.

"You're always in such a hurry to leave it, though."

Crap. That was meant to come out like jaunty banter, but instead it falls flat and sits in a sad little puddle between us. I smile too brightly and wish he'd offer me a splash of something in my mug to give me a little Dutch courage. He leans his head on his fist and his blue eyes burn bright.

"Would you like to stay with me tonight?"

I clear my throat and nod, tongue-tied. It's the first time he's ever asked. Usually, there is grinding and groping and tacit agreement, and we stagger home and fall into bed. I have no idea why tonight is so different, but then I suppose I initiated a different protocol, with the stalking and all.

"Stand up." His voice is soft, low and firm. I lean over to put my cup on the table and uncurl my legs. I pull myself to my feet and look down at him. "What is it you want, tonight, Cally?" The question paralyzes me. I've no smart answer because for once it doesn't really seem to be a smart question. I wrestle with the fear that I shouldn't be there, the conviction I'd had that I was chasing my tail. I open my mouth, and close it again. He sighs, but not irritably. "There's something I've been wanting to do all night."

He stands up and walks over to me. Putting his hands under the shoulder straps of my dress, he slips it down to my waist and inches it around and replaces it so the high front is at the back, and my front is…backless. My nipples pebble under the air and exposure and self-consciousness. He's framed my breasts like they're a painting and sat back down to look at it. "Will you take your boots off, Cal?" I nod. I bend and unlace my right boot, fumbling with the knot; the eyelets seem endless. I stand and balance myself to shuck it, kick it under the table and this time prop my left foot on the table. With my leggings on I'm still quite modest, or would be if my chest wasn't naked. I get the other boot off more quickly and drop it with a clunk. The noise makes me giggle: there's no question these are *fuck-you* boots, but Rob doesn't seem to mind, judging by the look in his eye.

He gestures, and I slide the leggings and underwear off myself and toss them onto the sofa. "What do you want, pretty girl in my living room?" I resist the urge to um and blush and I walk over to his chair.

"I want to be closer to you."

He holds a hand out to me, and I climb onto his lap. As I do, he reaches up and palms my breast and pulls me in.

"Well?"

"You usually...you don't usually ask, you just take," I whisper, leaning into his hands, arranging myself so I'm strad-dling his thigh, shivering with the chill on my bare skin and the contrasting heat of his hands.

"Well, you've never shown up at my door before." He lets me tip his face toward me and find his mouth with mine. His lips are firm and full and I can feel his sandy beard scratching at my face. He tastes familiar when I flick my tongue across his. Little shivers fill me at the connection. He hooks a finger into the strand of beads at my neck and starts to pull. Caught in my dress, they come slowly, snaggingly over my shoulders, then faster as there's more slack. They fall between my breasts and he fists them loosely in one hand and rubs the sliding mass of them over my exposed and eager tits. The beads are cool on my nipples. I close my eyes and breathe deeply. Rob pulls me forward by the necklace and loops it tight around my throat. He still has plenty to hold on to. The strand around my neck is taut, but I can still breathe, and I suck in air sharply when he catches my nipple in the fistful of beads he's holding and closes his hand. The beads crush together around it with tiny shrill noises and I feel a multitude of little points of pain light up on my tender flesh. I squeak and try to pull away, but the choke chain he's made of my necklace doesn't make that any more comfortable. He pulls me back in and does the same thing to the other nipple, reaching up to kiss me again as he pinches my delicate skin. The beads are light, but they have a multitude of edges that pinch and grind. I moan in protest but I don't move again. "What do you want?" he whispers into my ear.

"You?" I try, mashing my crotch against his jean-clad leg. He trails his fingers down my thigh and strokes my bare pussy. I tilt to let his fingers in and even at this awkward angle they fill me. I thrust onto them but he slides them out of me, trails them up through the beads, which tinkle and whisper as he goes, and pushes them into my mouth. This. I want this. The taste of him in my mouth, tart with a slick of my cream, this is exactly what I want.

"Ass on the table." Rob moves forward with ease, pushing me back until my legs hit the table, and I sit, more abruptly than I would like to. He slips to his knees and puts his mouth to the nipples he's just finished abusing. Lightning darts of pleasure zing around my body as he eases me backward, and pushes the skirt of my dress out of the way. He nuzzles my inner thigh, all soft lips and prickling beard, then his lips move slowly up to my cunt. I open for him and whimper when his tongue delves deep into me before licking up to my clit. His mouth feels so firm, so wet, his mustache and stubble press into my soft flesh and the burn drives the pleasure upward. My hand settles on the back of his head, winding tight into his thick hair as he starts a steady rhythm, building pressure, sucking on my aching, swelling, throbbing flesh until my abdomen begins to tighten and contract. And then he stops.

"What! What? Rob!"

"What do you want, Cally?" He rests his head on my thigh and begins to play with my cunt, just lightly, running his fingers up and down my lips, spreading the wetness around.

"I...I want to come! Rob, please!" I try to grind against him, but to no avail. He moves away and lifts my hips, flipping me over onto my front. The smooth wood of the table is cold against my breasts and belly and I shiver. Rob hunkers down beside me and whispers in my ear.

"Not until you give me what I'm looking for, baby. Now, remember that time we played with the hairbrush?" I gulp. "Hmm?" He smoothes my hair off my face so he can see me, and I nod.

"Yes." It comes out as a whisper.

"And you remember we agreed on a word you'd use if you needed things to stop or slow down?" I nod again, caught in the bright blue of his eyes. My face flushes but my pussy is flooding with the excitement and fear of anticipation, too. "Do I need to tie you down, Cal?" I really don't know if he does or not.

"No?"

He pats me on the head. I try to feel indignant, but it doesn't work. His fingertip trails all the way down my spine and taps three times. A beat, and his hand cracks onto my asscheek. It sparks and burns and I moan and put my head down and wait for the next one. He smacks me and waits, timing each pause just long enough to make me fear the next one, make me long for it. My pussy throbs and flames along with my ass.

I want his face back there. Even better, I want him to fuck me now. But he doesn't. He stops his punishment and strokes my hot cheeks. I groan and writhe back against him, but he just smacks me once more.

"Up. Bedroom." I scramble, slither off the table, melted and liquid and eager. He leads me into his room. It's white, mostly. The floor is stained dark, and the bed is dark wood, but everything else seems white in the dim light. I clamber onto the bed and as I make to turn around he catches my wrists and stretches them in front of me. Beneath the pillows are straps! I didn't notice them the time I was here. Velcro straps he fastens me into. My arms are spread wide and my head is low to the bed. He pushes my ass up high and checks my pussy. His fingers stroke, then enter again; he pushes against my G-spot. "What do you want, Cal?"

I groan in frustration. Isn't it obvious?

"I want you to fuck me, Rob, please." It's a good enough position to beg from. Being tipped up onto my face and spread open like this always undoes me. I can't think of much else but his cock at this point. But he's having none of it. He pulls his fingers out of me, leaving me gasping at the cold absence of his hand. He crawls to sit beside me and pushes my hair out of the way, touches my lips again. All of a sudden he smacks my face, not so hard, but I startle and try to jerk away. The straps mean I'm not going anywhere, and he does it again, a little harder.

"What do you want, Cal?"

"Ow!" I'm not used to this, and I'm shocked. I feel completely helpless, and small. He smacks me again and the side of my face stings. Before I can even analyze my reaction, I start to cry. Wet, lonely tears run from my eyes and he wipes them away—and smacks my face again, lazily.

"What?"

I'm spread open, and within a few minutes, he's put me in a place I could never access by myself.

"More." It comes out as a hoarse whisper. I press my face into the pillow as best I can.

"Oh, honey. It's okay, we've just begun. I can do this all night."

I sob and shake my head. "No, *more*. I want more. Than this. I want *you*."

"Ohhh." He moves his hand over my breasts, spreads it on my stomach.

"I want breakfast. Television. I don't want to have to go home." I start to babble. His hips press against my thighs and I can feel him lean to the side. I hear a condom packet rip and his hands leave me for a second and maneuver the rubber on. His cock presses against my open, wanting cunt and for a second I'm worried he didn't understand. But as he pushes into me he leans over and kisses my back, touches his forehead to my skin. His cock feels so good inside me that I almost don't care if that's all he's offering, but he leans over me and reaches for the straps, pulls my hands free. He pulls me up to his chest while he thrusts into me and wraps long arms round my torso, crossing my breasts and stomach. I am penetrated and held, it feels like flying, like floating.

"Is that what you want?" he whispers in my ear, licking the curves of my ear between sentences. I try to answer, but now the tip of his tongue is running electric shivers between every tiny hair inside my ear, hot as he exhales, cool as he pulls his breath away. His pubic hair bristles against my sore ass. He's pounding against that swelling wall inside and one big hand is pressing on my clit, rubbing as he fucks me. I'm trapped and there's no escape from the waves of pleasure that burst through me. He pinches my tender nipple and I reach back to hold on to his arm as I come, the heat and hurt and tightness of it shaking me.

We collapse to the bed, and he pulls me to his chest, arms around me. "It's what I want, too," he says, deep voice in my ear as I start to float away. "Sleep. And in the morning, there will be more."

TWO A.M.
DATE NIGHT

Sophia Valenti

Brandon was waiting for me when I got home. I'd been expecting to find him in the living room, but the sight of his silhouette, backlit by the street lamps shining through the window, still made me jump. My husband seemed so imposing sitting in the shadows, or perhaps it was the apprehension growing inside me that was making me feel so jittery.

"Hey," I called out into the darkness, my faltering voice betraying my nerves.

"Finally decided to come home, did you?" he answered, his tone sending a delicious shiver down my spine.

"Sorry. I know I'm late, but dinner took longer than expected—"

"It's two a.m., Celia," he interrupted. "Dinner was over hours ago."

He was right. I'd had a dinner date with Rick, an ex-boyfriend with whom I was still friendly. Well, more than friendly. Despite the fact that I'd been married to Brandon for more than a year, my sexual attraction to Rick was still strong, even though my motivation for hooking up with him was now very different.

While Rick and I were dating, we'd fucked like wildcats, but once our clothes were back on, we could never find a way to get along. I'd once joked with a girlfriend that Rick wasn't the type of boy you married. So I didn't, and chose Brandon instead—a man whom I could love and trust, and who satisfied me in ways Rick never could.

"What have you been doing all this time?"

"I was with Rick."

We both knew the real answer, but making me tell him was part of our game. However, it didn't matter how many times we'd played like this. It didn't make it any easier for me to confess. Even though I'd gone to see Rick with Brandon's blessing, the chill in my husband's voice made me feel as though I'd done something wrong—something that I needed to be punished for—and it was no coincidence that Brandon felt the same way.

"With Rick? Or *fucking* Rick?" Brandon stood, and I heard the click of his belt buckle as he unfastened it.

"F-f-fucking Rick." I nearly lost my place in our usual script when I heard the zip of his belt being pulled free. I'd been expecting Brandon to take me over his lap and spank me—not whip me with his belt. My throat tightened, but the thought of leather lashing my skin excited me, causing yet another complex mix of emotions to swirl through me.

As panicked as I was, I knew Brandon wouldn't actually hurt me. No, I take that back—he *would* hurt me, but in the best possible way. That I knew. He always pushes me to my limit, and then asks me to take a bit more—bending but never breaking me. His spankings are hard and fierce, but as much as I dread being taken over his lap, I also crave the sting of his hand. Just as I also crave the intense sex that follows and how he makes me come harder than any other man I've known. Even as I'm enjoying the sensation of Rick's thick cock filling my cunt, I'm imagining how Brandon will punish me for fucking him when I get home. But I'll never tell my lover that's the reason why my orgasms are so intense. You see, even when I'm with Rick, Brandon is in my head, controlling how I climax and making me long for the sweet pain that I know he'll deliver. I love it and hate it all at the same time, and at that moment, I couldn't deny that my pussy felt hot and slick. It didn't matter that I'd come thirty minutes earlier; I was hungry for more—hungry for the release that only Brandon could give me.

My husband moved closer to me in the darkness, like a predator slowly stalking his prey. "I have such a bad girl for a wife," he said, stroking my cheek with the back of his hand. I shivered at his touch, so soft and gentle. I shivered because I knew what those hands could do—how hard they could strike my bare ass, how they could easily capture my wrists in their unyielding grip. Each scene Brandon and I have together lays down another memory, and those moments linger in my mind and echo in my body, making every experience more intense than the last. "Such a bad, slutty girl," Brandon muttered, almost to himself. His voice sounded dreamy, and I instinctively knew he was picturing me and my lover. It was a thought that taunted and aroused him all at the same time.

Brandon slipped his hand inside my dress and into my bra, cupping my breast and running his thumb back and forth over my nipple. It perked up instantly, and he toyed with it absentmindedly as he continued. "Did you manage to make it back to his place? Or did he start fingering you in the restaurant?"

Brandon knows me too well.

"In the restaurant."

He pinched my nipple hard, and I gasped. "In the restau-rant—*what*?" he demanded, twisting my erect nub. The spark of pain encouraged me to spill the details.

"I wasn't wearing panties," I sputtered. "So during dessert, Rick slipped his hand up my dress and started fingering my pussy while I sat at the table."

"You went out to dinner without underwear, like a little slut?" Brandon queried, giving my nipple another harsh tug. A small sob escaped my lips, and my cunt felt like it was dripping.

"Y-y-yes, like a slut." As the word *slut* left my lips, I felt another rush of wetness seep from my pussy.

"And then what happened?"

"He took me back to his apartment, and we barely made it in the door before he tore off my dress. He couldn't wait to get me naked." I sighed as Brandon released my throbbing nipple, only to gasp again when he pinched the other, rolling it between his fingers and tugging it until I whimpered. I took a deep breath and continued to speak. I knew that was what Brandon wanted. It was what I wanted, too.

"He took off all my clothes and had me kneel on the couch—"

"Show me. Show me how." Brandon reached over and clicked on a small lamp. That's when I saw the animalistic desire in his ice-blue eyes. His black hair was disheveled, and his button-down shirt was partially open, revealing a muscular chest that was covered with swirls of dark hair. My eyes trav-eled downward to find the bulge of his erect cock in his faded jeans—and the thick black belt in his hand. I could barely take my eyes off the doubled-up loop of leather. The sight of it made my cunt ache.

I pulled my dress off over my head, but left on my red lace bra. The straps had slid down my shoulders, and my breasts hung out of the peeled-down cups, just as Brandon had left them—and just as Rick had done hours ago. Keeping on my high heels, I knelt on the black cushions with my thighs spread wide, grabbing the back of the velvet sofa. My long brown hair spread out across my back, the curls tickling my hypersensitive flesh. I could feel the cool air wafting over my exposed cunt, making me even more aware of how vulnerable I was.

Brandon approached me from behind, leaning over me and pressing himself against me. I shivered despite the warmth his body imparted to mine. "And what did he do once he had you naked?" Brandon ran his fingers along the front of me—between my breasts, along my stomach and over my mound—taking a leisurely trip downward, and then softly, slowly circling my swollen clit. I just barely stifled a whimper as Brandon's hand abandoned my pussy and he backed away, which I recognized as my sign to continue my X-rated tale.

"He trailed kisses down my back as he played with my cunt."

I felt a rush of air behind me and then the sting of the belt as it landed on my upturned ass. I inhaled abruptly and threw back my head, looking toward the ceiling with wide eyes as if searching for escape, but I knew there was none to be had. Excitement coursed through me, knowing there was no way out. Brandon was going to thrash me good. I was overwhelmed by emotion—and thoroughly turned on.

"I was so wet for him. His fingers were making squishing noises as they thrust in and out of me," I confessed, nearly panting.

The belt landed again and again in quick strikes, taking my words away from me. The loud report shocked me as much as the sensation did, but what shocked me most was that I wanted more. Even though it hurt, even though my face heated with shame, I was so aroused that I felt as if I were flying.

186 MORNING, NOON AND NIGHT

"You were so wet because you're a bad girl who lets men play with your cunt, even though you're married." Brandon interspersed his words with hot licks of the belt. With each lash, I squealed and tried to hold my position, but it was impossible. I lost my sense of time, my sense of self. I spread my thighs wider and thrust my ass upward, almost as if I were offering him more flesh to hit, to spread out the stinging slashes of leather and weaken their cumulative impact. Brandon accepted the invitation, lowering his aim and snapping the belt against the underside of my cheeks, first the left and then the right. He alternated between the two until my head dropped and I released a strangled cry. That's when he stopped, only to drag his fingernails up one asscheek and down the other, making me gasp. The leather's lingering sting radiated a pulsing heat that had spread to my pussy. My neglected clit throbbed, even as tears welled in my eyes.

Brandon was close behind me again, leaning down to whisper in my ear. "Did he make you come right away, or did you have to wait?"

"I had to wait because he wanted to fuck me first." Brandon ground his erection into my asscheeks, and the rough texture of his jeans against my well-whipped ass made me groan. My skin was so tender, and my cunt was aching with longing. He reached around my hip to stroke my slit again, and by this time I was so wet I was embarrassed. I was embarrassed that being abused this way turned me on so much, but there was nothing I could do to stop it.

Brandon's fingers lingered between my legs, stroking me casually, toying with my slick opening and venturing upward to circle my clit lazily. His touch was light and teasing—a remarkable contrast to how heavy-handed he was with the belt.

"Did he keep you positioned like this?" Brandon moved

back and lowered his zipper, and I heard the rustle of fabric as he freed his dick.

"Yes," I managed to utter. "Because he—" I stopped myself, hesitant to reveal more, perhaps because I knew where it would lead.

"What?" Brandon insisted as he ran his cockhead up and down my slippery slit—up and down, over and over, teasing me with the promise of penetration and release. I arched my back, offering myself to him silently. I was begging him with my body not to ask the question, just as much as I was begging him for satisfaction. "Tell me, Celia," he insisted.

"He wanted to finger my asshole while he fucked my pussy," I finally answered with a sob, feeling my face heat and my cunt clench.

As the words left my lips, Brandon shoved his cock into me in one hard thrust. "Oh, you're such a dirty, dirty girl," he sighed, taking one of his juice-slick fingers and circling it around my asshole as he plunged his shaft in and out of my cunt. He worked his dick in long firm strokes, jamming it into me fast and hard as I squeezed my muscles around him. As he continued pumping his hips, he slid his finger into my back hole, and I thrust toward him, impaling myself and filling both of my holes so sweetly. I moaned helplessly and wriggled in place.

"Did you take his cock up your ass?" Brandon asked, his voice a desperate-sounding hiss. I couldn't tell if I was hearing jealousy or lust—maybe it was a mixture of both.

"No."

"You're not lying, are you?" he asked, working another finger into my back hole.

"Oh—no, Brandon. No one's ever fucked me there. You know that." My words were whispers of astonishment.

"Then it's time someone does." Brandon yanked his cock

and fingers out of me, and I turned toward him in shock, but as I opened my mouth to argue, he grabbed me by the hair and looked me in the eyes.

"Your ass is mine—and I don't want to hear another word about it. Do you understand me?"

I nodded haltingly, not believing what I was agreeing to do.

"Good," he said, releasing my hair from his grip. "Now, you stay in position while I go get some lube. And god help you if you move—trust me, you won't be able to sit for a week."

Bound by his words, I held tight to the couch as I struggled to keep myself perfectly still. My ass was aching; I wasn't sure I could take another session with his belt so soon after the first. Deep down, I wasn't convinced he was serious, but I didn't want to take a chance. After all, Brandon had already surprised me more than once this evening.

I was grateful for the break, for the chance to steady my nerves and take a few deep breaths. I was in a heady sub space, feeling everything yet nothing. My thoughts were fuzzy, indistinct notions, and the real world seemed like fantasy.

Brandon didn't keep me waiting long, which was probably a good thing. Any more time and I might have lost my nerve. But even if I did, it was clear to me that he wasn't going to let me back out, and I would have expected nothing less—and that's one of the reasons I love him so much.

"Seems like you're getting better at following orders," he whispered in my ear upon his return. I didn't answer him, didn't dare look over my shoulder. But I didn't need to see him to know that he'd stripped himself naked. I could tell his clothes were gone because of the feeling of his muscular body pressed up against me and his erection nudging my tingling asscheeks. That brief touch of his hard cock made me aware of how much I wanted it inside me. Sure, I'd had a quick, pleasant climax at

Rick's hands, but he never truly satisfies me the way Brandon does. Even as my bottom burned and my stomach fluttered with nerves, in my head I was already striving for that perfect orgasm that would shake me to my core, soothing and satisfying me until I floated away on a cloud of bliss.

Brandon snapped me back to reality with another command: "I want you to hold your cheeks apart for me so I can lube you up."

"Brandon—" I started to protest, feeling my face heat with embarrassment. Somehow baring myself to him in this way seemed much more dirty than being taken. I wasn't sure I could do it.

"Get your hands back here and part your pretty cheeks so I can make your hole nice and slick." He punctuated his sentence with a hard slap to my ass, and I gasped at the impact. "Unless you want me to go ahead as is," he added matter-of-factly.

"No! I'll do it!" I said. My voice was so high-pitched it nearly squeaked.

Resting my head on the back of the couch, I reached back to do as he ordered. My asscheeks felt hot to the touch, and I clasped one in each hand, reawakening the burn as I clutched them, parting them for him. I had my eyes shut tight; I couldn't believe I was doing this.

"Ahh, that's perfect." Brandon took an extraordinarily long amount of time to admire me, and I was mortified. No one had ever had me positioned like this: bottom whipped and cheeks parted as I waited to have my ass violated. I was indignant, angry with him for pushing me, but I also couldn't wait to feel his cock filling me back there.

"You stay just like that," he whispered, drizzling lube between my cheeks. The cool liquid ran down my crack and over my back hole, tickling and teasing me. He nudged my opening with a single finger, gradually working it inside my ass. It was quickly followed by a second and a third, and then he moved them in and out slowly.

"Tell me you want it, Celia."

"I want it," I whispered, with my eyes closed and my face buried in the couch cushions. Nerves and fear be damned, it was the truth—even though I still was having trouble admitting it.

Brandon kept sliding his fingers in and out of me, his voice sounding as patient as a schoolteacher's. "You want what?"

"You—your cock—in my ass," I stuttered. "Please, Brandon."

Brandon pulled his fingers free, and I nearly sobbed when I felt the emptiness. I soon heard the sound of the lube bottle being squeezed again, and seconds later Brandon was rubbing his cockhead up and down my crack.

"I bet Rick wanted to do this tonight, to be the one to fuck your ass for the very first time," he said, increasing the pressure of his cock against my hole. "But it's all for me because you're my bad girl." I bit my lip as he pressed his dick against my back door, working through the last bit of my resistance. I grabbed my cheeks more tightly as he pressed forward and popped inside.

"Yes, Brandon. I'll always be yours," I whispered, my words floating away on a sigh of pleasure as he slowly sank into me.

"I'll take it from here," he said softly, moving my hands away and then grabbing my hips. The heady sensation of his cock plundering my tight hole overwhelmed me, and I was glad my hands were free to search for purchase amongst the cushions.

At first I let Brandon set the pace as he leisurely stroked in and out of me. But when he reached around to strum my clit, I began working my hips in little circles in a desperate attempt to increase the friction against my swollen button. My moves gradually became more frenzied, to the point where Brandon was nearly still. He let me control the action, thrusting back against him to fill my ass with his cock, only to rock forward again in order to press my clit against his fingertips. I rocked and rolled and rode the swelling wave of pleasure until I surrendered to an exquisite blast of ecstasy. Brandon soon followed suit, pumping into me as he clutched my hips and softly moaned my name as if it were some sort of orgasmic mantra.

Afterward, he clutched my sweaty body to his, struggling to speak. "So when are you seeing Rick again?" Brandon asked breathlessly, his voice tinged with hope.

"Next Saturday."

"Good—I can't wait."

THREE A.M. LAST CALL

Alison Tyler

I want the bartender to close and lock the front door of the bar. "What happens in The Local stays in The Local" I want some wiseass to say. There will be laughter, of the nervous variety, and the men will try not to look into each other's eyes. Because what we're going to do here is a gang bang, and brother, when you say those words aloud, people get jittery.

This isn't noncon, mind you. I am not asking for something from *Last Exit to Brooklyn*. Don't leave me unconscious on an old vinyl car seat behind the bar. Yes, I want the abuse, but I want to revel in every moment. In fact, I want to name the lineup. That's why we have to wait until closing time, when everyone else can leave except for the five men I've chosen.

Choosing was the difficult part. Which five? And even more curious—*why* five? Five is the number I've decided on tonight because I think that's what I can take. Five guys in a line. One after the other. Or five guys in a circle, coming on my naked skin.

I won't start out naked. I want to be clothed and mussed. I

want my opaque black tights pulled down, my panties tugged until the seams give way. This outfit was purposefully chosen for the thin material that will tear easily. I would have worn a dress made of paper if one were readily available.

Closing time's coming. I look at the clock over the bar. The boys are starting to shuffle around. I can tell that they want the rest of the crowd to leave as much as I do. *Stumble home, people. Get into your trucks, shut one eye, and hope you make the ride home alive. However you do it, get the fuck out.* My five are all hard. I can tell. They are about to come in their pants, and we haven't even started.

How did I choose the team?

Number one goes without saying. He's my man. Declan wants this to happen as much as I do. We talk about nothing else when we're in bed, his hand on my throat, his cock to the hilt inside me. "How many can you take?" he likes to ask. "Could you do three? Four? How many could you work, baby?"

Tonight, we're finally going to find out.

Next up? The bartender. He's young yet, and baby-faced. He thinks he's all that and a bag of chips. Why shouldn't he? The girlies in town take their turns riding his cock and his pretty blond mustache. But we're going to age him tonight.

The chef—if you can call him that, more of a fry cook—he's third. Why? Because the big guy seems lonely, and I've always been a compassionate sort. He's good-looking, with an extra solid forty pounds on his six-foot frame and a guilty look in his eyes all the time. What type of porn does he have stashed under his single twin? I'd like to know.

Fourth is a friend going through the type of divorce that makes men believe all women are cunts. Flynn is bitter and angry. I want him to take that aggression out on me. *Call me her name*, I plan on telling him. *Make it hurt.*

Five is a drifter. He's not a local. But he's the kind of guy who has always made me perk up and take notice. He's lean and hard-bodied in his old buffalo-plaid flannel shirt and worn Levi's. He looks as if he has done some serious fighting in his life—hands all scarred to shit—but he also has that glint in his eyes. Yeah, he's done some serious fucking, as well.

The other four know that this is a gang bang. The drifter? I simply asked if he'd stay on after closing. He gave me a look of mild interest, tracing me up and down with his dark blue eyes, and said he didn't have anywhere better to be.

How can we do a gang bang in a small town like ours? We're all friends here. Or if not friends, at least not enemies. We all know each other. That's my point. This could be a problem in some places. How can I sashay in next Friday night after having been spread out on the pool table tonight, whipped and fucked by neighbors?

Like I said, tonight we're finally going to find out.

Here's my thought on the matter: We all know each other's secrets here. Why not add one more? Look, I don't want to be one of those women who reaches the end of her road and thinks, *Why not? What the fuck was I waiting for?* I want to sit there on my front porch in my rocker and have shimmering nights like these to remember.

The regulars are starting to leave. Last call ends the show. My five are shifting. Yeah, they're hard. All of them. The chef keeps stepping forward and peering through the doorway from the kitchen. The bartender drops a glass, something I've never seen him do before. My man has his hand on my waist, his mouth on my neck. He's kissing me and telling me how fucking sexy I am and how proud of me he is. Our buddy, touching the spot where his ring used to be, looks as if he can't wait to come in my face and make me like it. And the drifter? He toys with his half-empty shot glass on the bar, clearly waiting to take his cues from the rest of us.

Say you want a guy to tie you up, and you might win a raised eyebrow. Ask for a spanking, and there's a pussy type of man who will raise his hand—not to smack your ass, but in protest— and tell you he doesn't go in for that sort of thing. But confess that what you really desire, what keeps you up in the night, is to have a line of men take turns fucking you, and you'll find out who your friends truly are.

The bar's quiet now. The door is locked, front light out. We're all sitting exactly where we were when Brody hollered "Last call." Then the cook comes out to lean against the bar. He grips a beer in one big mitt and stares at me. The bartender, always so damn cocky in the past, lifts a bottle of vodka from the shelf and pours himself a shot on the largish side. Declan starts to kiss me, his mouth hot on mine, his hands roaming over my body. I'm sitting next to his buddy, Flynn, and I feel Flynn move in tighter to me. We haven't talked rules—because how can you do that? How can you run down the rules to a gang bang if you've never participated in one before? I have the feeling that this is the sort of activity that grabs momentum as the event progresses. Because right now, there's just Declan kissing me and Flynn's hands on my body.

Oh, wait. *That's* new. Flynn is running his hands along my back while Declan kisses my neck. I have my eyes closed until the scrape of a chair catches my attention. Is it the cook coming closer? The drifter taking off? No, it's Brody, setting upside-down chairs onto the nearby tables, as if this were any other closing night on any other night of the week.

But it's not. Flynn lifts my hair and starts to kiss the nape of my neck. A shiver works through me. The cook walks closer to us. He says, "Did you mean what you said before?"

What'd I say before? You're wondering, aren't you? I'd leaned in while he was cooking, and I waited until he looked my way. Then I said, "Joe, you've always wanted to fuck me, haven't you?"

People don't get to talk like that very often. Do you know what I mean? Most of the day, we walk around stifling our inner selves, damping down on the words we'd love to let loose. But I thought, *Fuck that. Tonight, I'm going to get what I want or flame out trying.* Joe had looked at me and said, "Hell yeah, Dina. You break up with Dec yet?"

When I shook my head, his eyebrows shot up, and I simply said, "If you're game, stay on after closing." Declan had a similar convo with Brody. And now we're all here, and Flynn has moved me onto the closest table, and Declan is pushing my dress to my hips and Brody's coming forward, clearly unsure what to do, but not so unsure he won't make a move. He's young, but he's a bartender. He's had his share of girls.

"This an every Friday night occasion?" That's the drifter. He's smoking even though you're not allowed to smoke in a bar in California anymore. But we've got bigger secrets to keep than that.

"No," says Declan, "Not every Friday." And I giggle because I can't help myself. I'm spread on a table, soft woven dress to my hips, Joe stroking my hair off my face, Flynn surprisingly gentle with his mouth on my fingertips. And this drifter wants to know if we do this all the time.

Flynn takes my hand and places my palm against the bulge in his slacks. When was the last time I touched another man's cock? A man aside from my husband? More than ten years. I trace my fingers along the rise of his erection, and I sigh because this is happening. Finally and for real.

I cup his balls through his jeans, and Flynn presses forward to gain more contact. I wonder for a second if I'm going to be graceful enough to figure this out. I've never had much rhythm. But then Brody kisses me, moving aside Flynn and Declan. He leans down and kisses me, and I think that I don't have to worry so much after all. The guys will do all the shifting and choreographing for me. I let myself go in the kiss. I kiss him the way I have always wanted to, every time I walk into the bar. Because girls want things, too. Guys don't hold the patent on lusting after what you're not supposed to have. I sigh as he pulls away, and I close my eyes.

When you're single, you can walk into a bar and pick your man. You can make eyes at the bartender. You can flirt with the chef. You can focus on a drifter and decide that yeah, maybe tonight you'll sample a bit of strange. There's excitement on every horizon. How will that bartender fuck you? Bent over a bar stool? In his pickup truck? Out in the woods, where nobody can hear? What does the fry cook like to watch when nobody's home? Man-on-man porn, right? He'll let you lick his asshole and fuck him with a strap-on, so long as you don't tell anyone later. And the drifter? Oh, I miss my one-night stands with the men passing through. Men whose names I'd forget later, but I'd remember the connection. And maybe a flicker or two of something else. Like finding a hidden scar way up high under a shirt sleeve. Or seeing a girl's name tattooed somewhere sacred.

But when you're part of the old-and-married club, the tools get rusty. You're not supposed to want to fuck anyone else, anymore, ever again. Take your libido, honey. Bottle it up in that mason jar and stick the thing on a shelf. No more surprises for you, dearie. You're all used up.

Things start to move faster now. I think Declan has been waiting for someone to show a sign of life, and that someone is

Brody. Brody, whose kiss I still feel on my lips, the taste of his vodka on my tongue.

I sense the men moving around me. Declan tells me to open my mouth, and I do, not surprised at all to find a naked cock at my lips. I keep my eyes closed still, as if I have a blindfold on, because it's still easier that way. I know right away that it's Declan's cock I'm sucking. After more than a decade together, I am well versed in the girth and the ridges that make this cock feel like home to me. I suck him on my back. He lets me work at my own pace. Then I moan—I can't help myself—because there's a mouth between my legs, on my pussy through my panties and my hose.

Who is that? I would like to know, would like to peek, but in this position, even if I opened my eyes, I'd only have a view of cock and balls.

"Put out your hands," Declan says, and I realize I have my fists clenched tight at my sides. I spread my arms open, palms open, and in seconds I have a dick in each hand. Am I stroking off Flynn? Jerking off the stranger? I don't look. I don't ask. My tights are getting wet in the center. The man between my legs is sucking at the nylon.

I sense the hesitation and then Declan says, "Take them off her."

My heels are pulled off, and then the hose. I shiver at the feeling of another man taking off my clothes. It hasn't happened in so fucking long. Then I feel a mustache against my thigh, and I know that's Brody between my legs. How funny that I've always yearned for a mustache ride, and now I'm getting my wish. His whiskers are sweet against my naked skin, his mouth warm and open over my panties. Declan moves and I open my eyes and blink. I am looking up into the eyes of Joe the chef and the nameless drifter. Joe's got a cock like I thought he would have.

Thick and long and hard. It suits him. The drifter's is thinner, but rigid. I was wrong. Flynn isn't close by. He's standing back, watching. His eyes are wet.

"Get her naked," Declan says.

Brody pulls my panties down then, and I raise my hips to help him, but I don't stop stroking those cocks. I feel energized, as if I could do this all night. The low, hungry sighs of the men is payment enough. I am the center, the focus of attention, and I bask in the glow.

Brody dives back between my thighs, and I bend my knees and splay for him, back arching. He's so good. Declan knows how to eat me, knows all the tricks and turns I love best. But there's something unreal about having that magic mustache run over my pussy lips and against my inner thighs.

Then suddenly, Flynn is in motion. "If we're going to do this, we should really do this," he says, surprising me. He's not my husband. But he takes charge, nonetheless, gripping me in his arms and carrying me to a low, heavy wooden table in the back of the room. He pulls my dress off me, leaving me totally naked. Then he motions to Brody, who gets on the table first as if he and Flynn have had a private conversation, and then he positions me over Brody's mouth, on my hands and knees.

"Like that," he says as Brody resumes licking my pussy. "You," he points to Joe. "You start."

"Start?" Joe's cock is in his hand. He's jerking it as he talks.

"Let her suck you."

Joe looks to Declan, who nods, and then he steps forward. I part my lips and take him in. He's so nice and thick. I suck him as sweetly as I can, thinking of how lonely he seems, how needy. I make the most of the seconds he's in my mouth before

Flynn grabs his shoulders and says, "Now fuck her."

For a second, everything stops, even Brody's tongue on my clit. There's an edge to Flynn's tone. But maybe we needed this. Someone to take command. Joe moves behind me and begins to slip his cock into my pussy. I'm swollen and wet. So wet. Brody continues to lick my clit as Joe fucks me. I turn my head and see that Declan is pressed back against the wall, watching everything.

Flynn grabs onto the drifter. "Now, you," he says. "What's your name?"

"Matthew."

"Matt, let her suck you."

The drifter gets in front of me, and I open my mouth for him. He looks over his shoulder, and I know he's getting approval from Declan. That he knows who the boss really is. His cock tastes like ocean water. I suck him to the rhythm that Joe is fucking me, to the beat that Brody is licking me and I groan at the sensation of being so well cared for.

Joe starts to speed up, and I realize he's going to come. He grips my hips and pounds into me, then pulls out at the last moment and shoots all over my back. I shiver at the sensation. I'm wearing another man's come. I wonder if someone will grab the bar towel, wipe me clean.

But Flynn is like a machine. He pulls Joe away, puts the drifter into place and then turns to look at Declan. "You up, man?"

Dec grins at him. "Flynn," he says in a kind voice, "I'm last."

The drifter is in my pussy, and his cock seems to reach further than Joe's did. I see Joe moving to pour himself a drink behind the bar. Flynn takes his spot in front of me. Brody is busy licking my clit like a good boy. Flynn strokes my hair and looks into my eyes. I was there on his wedding day. I was at his house when he found out his wife was cheating. I see all the pain in his eyes, and I see that he wants to imbue some of that onto me. And I want to take it.

The drifter drags his fingernails down my sides, and I shiver. He palms the cheeks of my ass, spreads them a bit to see my hole. I see him in the mirror as he motions to Joe, who is watching with a glass in hand.

"Come here," he says, and Joe walks closer. I watch in the mirror as Joe and Matthew kiss while Matthew's fucking me. He pulls out before coming, and the two start to make out against the wall, Matthew's dick shiny with my juices, Joe's big fist working around the shaft.

Flynn, who was gentle at the start, who was unsure for the first few minutes, begins to face-fuck me, and I never miss a beat. I suck him like a pro, and I'm pleased with myself. I drain him before he can stop himself from coming. I'm every woman he's ever loved, and every bitch he's ever hated, and he howls as he comes down my throat. There's no undoing that. Whenever he sees me from now on, he will own this moment. He backs off me, and he's no longer in charge.

Now there's Brody on the table and Declan stepping forward.

"Suck him," Dec says. "Suck his cock."

I undo Brody's jeans and set him free.

"Suck him while I fuck you," Dec instructs, and I do what he says, licking the precome from the head of Brody's cock and then sucking him while Declan takes his proper place behind me. Brody has to lean upward to keep contact with my clit, and I'm on my elbows with my ass in the air.

"You're so pretty," Declan says, and it's like there's only him and me in the room, except for the cock between my lips and the tongue on my clit. Except for the fact that Joe and Matthew are fucking against the bar and Flynn is lighting up one of Matthew's cigarettes.

Declan slaps my ass and grabs my hair. He fucks me hard, and I come, Brody licking my clit like a beast and then shooting into my mouth. I would collapse against the bartender, but Declan lifts me up, carries me to the hallway and presses me up against the wall. Now it is him and me, and he fucks me so hard, I feel like I've never been done before. Like this is the first time.

Which in a way it is.

The first gang bang. The first time I ever showed off who I really am deep inside. Dec comes in me and then spins me around and lifts me into his arms.

"The first of many," Dec promises with a smile.

ABOUT THE AUTHORS

PRESTON AVERY (prestonavery.com) lives merrily by the sea with her trusty laptop and the constant company of her slightly less trusty mutts, Bonnie and Clyde. She loves reading almost as much as writing and embraces both with reckless abandon. Feel free to get in touch! Twitter: twitter.com/Preston_Avery

VIDA BAILEY is a lady writer from Ireland who writes stories when the whim takes her. She has published work in *Love at First Sting*, *Dirtyville*, *Steamlust* and *Bound by Lust*. You can find her at www.heatsuffused.blogspot.com, where she blogs on occasion.

By day, **JAX BAYNARD** is a financial investment advisor. By night, she makes her own (and her clients') fantasies come true. This part-time dominatrix's short fiction has appeared in *With This Ring, I Thee Bed*, *Pleasure Bound*, online, and in several literary journals.

CHEYENNE BLUE's (cheyenneblue.com) erotica has appeared in over sixty anthologies including *Best Women's Erotica*, *Mammoth Best New Erotica*, *Cowboy Lust: Erotic Romance for Women* and *Lesbian Lust*. The darkness before dawn is her favorite time of day.

She's done it again! At thirty-eight, **ANGELL BROOKS** has somehow managed to fluke her way into another collection with some amazing erotica writers, and she couldn't be happier. The road trip to the top of the charts continues from Toronto, with dreams of tropical climates, cabana boys and tequila.

HEIDI CHAMPA (heidichampa.blogspot.com) has been published in numerous anthologies including *Best Women's Erotica 2010*, *Playing With Fire*, *Frenzy* and *Ultimate Curves*. She has also steamed up the pages of *Bust* magazine. Her work appears electronically at *Clean Sheets*, *Ravenous Romance*, *Oysters and Chocolate* and *The Erotic Woman*.

DANTE DAVIDSON's short stories have appeared in *Bondage*, *Naughty Stories from A to Z*, *Best Bondage Erotica*, *The Merry XXXmas Book of Erotica*, *Luscious* and *Sweet Life*. With Alison Tyler, he is the co-author of *Bondage on a Budget* and *Secrets for Great Sex After 50*.

JEREMY EDWARDS is the author of the erotocomedic novels *Rock My Socks Off* and *The Pleasure Dial*. His short stories have appeared in over fifty anthologies, including recent volumes in *The Mammoth Book of Best New Erotica* series. Readers can surprise him in his underwear at jeremyedwardserotica.com.

JUSTINE ELYOT (justineelyot.com) arrived on the erotica scene for the last gasp of Black Lace with her UK best seller *On Demand*. Since then, she has been published by a variety of imprints, including Carina Press, Xcite Books, Cleis Press and Total E-Bound, among others. Her website is regularly updated with details of her latest projects.

VICTORIA JANSSEN (victoriajanssen.com) has published three erotic novels with Harlequin Spice as well as many short stories. She's currently a regular blogger for both *Heroes & Heartbreakers* (romance) and *The Criminal Element* (mystery).

GEORGIA E. JONES graduated with an MFA from Mills College. Her stories have appeared in the *Santa Barbara Review*, *Alison's Wonderland* (Harlequin) and the literary magazine *Estero*. She lives in Northern California. Her novella *The Earl Takes a Lover* was published as a Harlequin Spice Brief.

ASHLEY LISTER is the UK author of more than two dozen full-length erotic titles and countless saucy short stories. Ashley's fiction has appeared in a range of magazines and anthologies including Maxim Jakubowski's Best Erotica series. When not writing fiction, Ashley works as a creative writing lecturer in the north west of England.

KRISTINA LLOYD (kristinalloyd.co.uk) is the author of three erotic novels including the controversial *Asking for Trouble*. Her short stories have appeared in numerous anthologies, including several "best of" collections, and her work has been translated into German, Dutch and Japanese. She has a master's degree in twentieth-century literature and lives in Brighton, UK.

SOMMER MARSDEN's short work has appeared in over 100 print anthologies. And she's not done yet. Sommer is the author of *Restless Spirit*, *Big Bad* and numerous other erotic novels. Visit her at sommermarsden.blogspot.com for more info on her work, her wiener [dog], her great lust for wine and unrequited love affair with running.

N.T. MORLEY is the author of twenty-four published novels of erotic dominance and submission, as well as short fiction that has appeared in many other anthologies—much of it collected in Morley's three published collections from Renaissance Ebooks. A complete bibliography and sales page can be found at ntmorley.com.

KATE PEARCE was born in England and spent much of her childhood living happily in a dream world. A move to the USA allowed her to fulfill her dreams and write her first novel. Kate is published by Signet Eclipse, Kensington Aphrodisia, Ellora's Cave, Cleis Press and Virgin Black Lace/Cheek.

TERESA NOELLE ROBERTS heeded that advice to write about what she knows, which means she's been published in *Best Bondage Erotica* 2011 and 2012, *Kinky Girls*, *Pleasure Bound* and dozens of other anthologies with blush-inducing titles. She also writes paranormal erotic romances, but she swears the paranormal part is purely imagination.

THOMAS S. ROCHE's novel *The Panama Laugh* was a finalist for the Horror Writers' Association's Bram Stoker Award. Roche's other books include the *Noirotica* series of erotic crime anthologies and four collections of fantasy and horror. A prolific blogger, Roche writes regularly for TinyNibbles.com, Boiled-Hard.com and many other blogs.

DONNA GEORGE STOREY (DonnaGeorgeStorey.com) enjoys watching football with her husband very much. Her adults-only tales have appeared in numerous places including *Best Women's Erotica, The Mammoth Book of Best New Erotica, Penthouse, Frenzy, Never Have the Same Sex Twice* and *Alison's Wonderland*. She is also the author of the erotic novel *Amorous Woman*.

SOPHIA VALENTI (sophiavalenti.blogspot.com) is the author of *Indecent Desires*, an erotic novella of spanking and submission, and her fiction has appeared in the anthologies *Alison's Wonderland* and *With This Ring, I Thee Bed*, as well as *Kiss My Ass, Skirting the Issue, Bad Ass* and *Torn*.

KAT WATSON (katwatson.com) is a mom, wife, crafter and chef. She enjoys all couplings and settings. Love is almost always the reason, but the surrounding details fascinate her. Figuring out the talking voices in her head is one of her greatest pleasures. Finding a fabulous bottle of red wine is, too.

AISLING WEAVER writes from a tower in a steel forest and in the belly of a sailboat. Her growing list of published work includes the novellas *Dedication* and *Finding Anastasia*. When not turning the pages of life, she can be found on her blog at AislingWeaver.com.

Gifted with a salacious imagination, national bestselling author **SASHA WHITE's** (sashawhite.net) brand of *Romance with Heat and Erotica with Heart* is all about sassy women and sexy men. With a voice that is called "distinctive and delicious" by the Romance Studio, this Canadian author has become a reader favorite.

CORA ZANE (CoraZane.com) lives in an area of northern Louisiana known as "out in the sticks." Her work has been published by Ellora's Cave, Cobblestone Press, Wild Child Publishing and various other independent and electronic publishers.

ABOUT
THE EDITOR

Called "a trollop with a laptop" by *East Bay Express*, "a literary siren" by Good Vibrations and "the mistress of literary erotica" by Violet Blue, **ALISON TYLER** is naughty and she knows it.

Over the past two decades, Ms. Tyler has written more than twenty-five explicit novels, including *Tiffany Twisted, Melt with You* and *The ESP Affair*. Her novels and short stories have been translated into Japanese, Dutch, German, Italian, Norwegian, Spanish and Greek. When not writing sultry short stories, she edits erotic anthologies, including *Alison's Wonderland, Kiss My Ass, Skirting the Issue* and *Torn*.

Ms. Tyler is loyal to coffee (black), lipstick (red) and tequila (straight). She has tattoos, but no piercings; a wicked tongue, but a quick smile; and bittersweet memories, but no regrets. She believes it won't rain if she doesn't bring an umbrella, prefers hot and dry to cold and wet, and loves to spout her favorite motto: You can sleep when you're dead. She chooses Led Zeppelin over the Beatles, the Cure over NIN, and the Stones over everyone.

Yet although she appreciates good rock, she has a pitiful weakness for '80s hair bands.

In all things important, she remains faithful to her partner of seventeen years, but she still can't choose just one perfume.

More from Alison Tyler

Frenzy
60 Stories of Sudden Sex
Edited by Alison Tyler

"Toss out the roses and box of candies. This isn't a prolonged seduction. This is slammed against the wall in an alleyway sex, and it's all that much hotter for it."
—Erotica Readers & Writers Association
ISBN 978-1-57344-331-9 $14.95

Best Bondage Erotica
Edited by Alison Tyler

Always playful and dangerously explicit, these arresting fantasies grab you, tie you down, and never let you go.
ISBN 978-1-57344-173-5 $15.95

Afternoon Delight
Erotica for Couples
Edited by Alison Tyler

"Alison Tyler evokes a world of heady sensuality where fantasies are fearlessly explored and dreams gloriously realized."
—Barbara Pizio, Executive Editor, *Penthouse Variations*
ISBN 978-1-57344-341-8 $14.95

Got a Minute?
60 Second Erotica
Edited by Alison Tyler

"Classy but very, very dirty, this is one of the few very truly indispensable filth anthologies around." —*UK Forum*
ISBN 978-1-57344-404-0 $14.95

Playing with Fire
Taboo Erotica
Edited by Alison Tyler

"Alison Tyler has managed to find the best stories from the best authors, and create a book of fantasies that—if you're lucky enough, or determined enough—just might come true." —Clean Sheets
ISBN 978-1-57344-348-7 $14.95

Read the Very Best in Erotica

Fairy Tale Lust
Erotic Fantasies for Women
Edited by Kristina Wright
Foreword by Angela Knight

Award-winning novelist and top erotica writer Kristina Wright goes over the river and through the woods to find the sexiest fairy tales ever written.
ISBN 978-1-57344-397-5 $14.95

In Sleeping Beauty's Bed
Erotic Fairy Tales
By Mitzi Szereto

"Classic fairy tale characters like Rapunzel, Little Red Riding Hood, Cinderella, and Sleeping Beauty, just to name a few, are brought back to life in Mitzi Szereto's delightful collection of erotica fairy tales."
—Nancy Madore, author of *Enchanted: Erotic Bedtime Stories for Women*
ISBN 978-1-57344-376-8 $16.95

Frenzy
60 Stories of Sudden Sex
Edited by Alison Tyler

"Toss out the roses and box of candies. This isn't a prolonged seduction. This is slammed against the wall in an alleyway sex, and it's all that much hotter for it."
—Erotica Readers & Writers Association
ISBN 978-1-57344-331-9 $14.95

Fast Girls
Erotica for Women
Edited by Rachel Kramer Bussel

Fast Girls celebrates the girl with a reputation, the girl who goes all the way, and the girl who doesn't know how to say "no."
ISBN 978-1-57344-384-5 $14.95

Can't Help the Way That I Feel
Sultry Stories of African American Love, Lust and Fantasy
Edited by Lori Bryant-Woolridge

Some temptations are just too tantalizing to ignore in this collection of delicious stories edited by Emmy award-winning and *Essence* bestselling author Lori Bryant-Woolridge.
ISBN 978-1-57344-386-9 $14.95

Many More Than Fifty Shades of Erotica

Please, Sir
Erotic Stories of Female Submission
Edited by Rachel Kramer Bussel

If you liked *Fifty Shades of Grey*, you'll love the explosive stories of *Yes, Sir*. These damsels delight in the pleasures of taking risks to be rewarded by the men who know their deepest desires. Find out why nothing is as hot as the power of the words "Please, Sir."
ISBN 978-1-57344-389-0 $14.95

Yes, Sir
Erotic Stories of Female Submission
Edited by Rachel Kramer Bussel

Bound, gagged or spanked—or controlled with just a glance—these lucky women experience the breathtaking thrills of sexual submission. *Yes, Sir* shows that pleasure is best when dispensed by a firm hand.
ISBN 978-1-57344-310-4 $15.95

He's on Top
Erotic Stories of Male Dominance and Female Submission
Edited by Rachel Kramer Bussel

As true tops, the bossy hunks in these stories understand that BDSM is about exulting in power that is freely yielded. These kinky stories celebrate women who know exactly what they want.
ISBN 978-1-57344-270-1 $14.95

Best Bondage Erotica 2012
Edited by Rachel Kramer Bussel

How do you want to be teased, tied and tantalized? Whether you prefer a tough top with shiny handcuffs, the tug of rope on your skin or the sound of your lover's command, Rachel Kramer Bussel serves your needs.
ISBN 978-1-57344-754-6 $15.95

Bottoms Up
Spanking Good Stories
Edited by Rachel Kramer Bussel

As sweet as it is kinky, *Bottoms Up* will propel you to pick up a paddle and share in both pleasure and pain, or perhaps simply turn the other cheek. This torrid tour de force is essential reading.
ISBN 978-1-57344-362-3 $15.95

Ordering is easy! Call us toll free or fax us to place your MC/VISA order.
You can also mail the order form below with payment to:
Cleis Press, 2246 Sixth St., Berkeley, CA 94710.

ORDER FORM

QTY	TITLE	PRICE
———	—————————————————	———
———	—————————————————	———
———	—————————————————	———
———	—————————————————	———
———	—————————————————	———
———	—————————————————	———
———	—————————————————	———
———	—————————————————	———

SUBTOTAL	———
SHIPPING	———
SALES TAX	———
TOTAL	———

Add $3.95 postage/handling for the first book ordered and $1.00 for each additional book. Outside North America, please contact us for shipping rates. California residents add 8.75% sales tax. Payment in U.S. dollars only.

* Free book of equal or lesser value. Shipping and applicable sales tax extra.

Cleis Press • Phone: (800) 780-2279 • Fax: (510) 845-8001
orders@cleispress.com • www.cleispress.com
You'll find more great books on our website

Follow us on Twitter @cleispress • Friend/fan us on Facebook